PRAISE FOR *BIRDIE*

"*Birdie* is many things: a sharp yet big-hearted story of resiliency and transformation, an intense psychological novel diffused across a group of like-minded Cree women, a vision quest with a twist. It's poetic and at times surreal, with short, potent fables and dream sequences bookending each chapter. And it's inventive, with a chronology that's more corkscrew than straight line, repeating familiar scenes in the protagonist's life but picking up new and vital details with each passing loop. The simple heart of the book, though, is Birdie herself."
— Michael Hingston, *Edmonton Journal*

"For those who take their humour black, *Birdie* can also be funny as hell. Bernice is witty, sardonic and downright snarky.... [Lindberg] deftly addresses the lack of national empathy toward aboriginal women by dodging cultural stereotypes and celebrating the contradictions that make Bernice human.... *Birdie* establishes Lindberg as an important new voice."
— *The Globe and Mail*

"Birdie is a contemporary hero, smart and funny even as she reaches her breaking point, and through Lindberg's thorough imagining of her, she becomes easy to know, even to love."
— *National Post*

"Twisting, darkly funny, heartbreaking, sometimes brilliant."
— *Publishers Weekly*

"Described as '*Monkey Beach* meets *The Beachcombers*,' so in case you think you're in for a laugh-a-minute quirky Canadian romp with Jesse, Relic and the gang, you're in for a treat. Because it's not that. It's more. It's more meaningful, truer, richer, deeper."
— *Villamere*

"[A] powerful debut novel. . . . [Lindberg] incorporates elements of Cree folklore and oral tradition into the narrative, adding a layer of richness and mythic resonance. Moreover, despite the seriousness of the material, there are often glints of an earthy, life-affirming humour. . . . *Birdie* is a stirring story—but not simply because it's an account of a character who overcomes adversity. It offers a more nuanced view of individual triumph. Tellingly, Bernice's recovery of self begins in solitude, when she withdraws into dreams. But it ultimately depends on taking her place in a community."   —*Toronto Star*

"A funny, sad and occasionally harrowing tale. . . . Bernice, or Birdie, is an intriguing protagonist who refuses to be defeated by a dark secret from her past."   —*Edmonton Journal*

"The richest and yet most hopeful exploration of sexual violence and the colonial condition that I have read."
            —Sherene Razack, award-winning author and editor of
            Race, Space and the Law: Unmapping a White Settler Society

"A stunning debut novel, grounded in the sheer beauty of Cree poetics, love, and a benevolence few of us are lucky enough to know. The brilliance of Indigenous women dances off each page—this story is our story, so carefully woven together into a tapestry that is the spine of our collective beings. I see myself, my family and my life in every sentence. This is the novel Canada has been waiting for."
            —Leanne Simpson, author of *Islands of Decolonial Love*

BIRDIE

BIRDIE

Tracey Lindberg

A NOVEL

HarperCollins*PublishersLtd*

Published by HarperCollins Publishers Ltd

First published in Canada by HarperCollins Publishers Ltd
in a hardcover edition: 2015
This HarperCollins trade paperback edition: 2016

HarperCollins books may be purchased for educational, business,
or sales promotional use through our Special Markets Department.

HarperCollins Publishers Ltd
2 Bloor Street East, 20th Floor
Toronto, Ontario, Canada
M4W 1A8

www.harpercollins.ca

Library and Archives Canada Cataloguing in Publication
information is available upon request.

ISBN 978-1-44345-135-2

Printed and bound in the United States of America
RRD 9 8 7 6 5 4 3

For Cindy

Kakinow anniki okawipanak, nimisinanak, niseeminanak, kaki mantotacik, apo anniki westawow mekwac eka ka piswenemicik, kiwicikapowistatinan, kakinow annis omma kiwakotonanow.

To all of the mothers and little mothers, sisters and cousins who are murdered, missing, disappeared or who feel invisible. We are one. We are with you. We are family.

CONTENTS

BERNICE'S JOURNEY

1. ~~Home~~ Loon Lake

2. Christly School and the Pecker Palace

3. Care: Ingelson family

4. Street life (Edmonton)

5. The San

6. ~~Lola's~~ Home

BIRDIE

Prologue

WHERE SHE IS NOW –
WHEN SHE MADE TWO JOURNEYS

ôtah mâcipayiw: It starts from here

MAGGIE SITS IN THE OLD TAVERN, amongst friends. The only spirits in the place, in the place with the endless celebration, are those that swirl around them, little tornadoes of light, laughter, love and grace. She reaches out and touches one, is lit up, feels her littlebigwomandaughter/mother and knows the love by heart. The sensation is one of satiation: full and fed. With the same light, laughter, love and grace. She was peaceful the moment she left. She is at peace when she touches the spirit she knows is in Bernice. Her girl is rich, rich with possibility and lifeforce. It fills Maggie and the room and everyone is awed for a moment while it passes through and over them. Her girl is filled with feelings that Maggie only gets to feel now, in this place.

She feelhears clatter and clapping as someone enters the bar. It's *Kohkom*, dressed for ceremony. With some red heels on, to boot.

And, ready to dance.

1

WHO SHE IS

nayahcikewiyiniw: a person who bears things on her/his back

pawatamowin*

In her dream, she's not in the lean-to in front of Pimatisewin,† *but in Gastown in Vancouver. She is flying in her nightie, through the cobbled streets, amazed by the smells of spices and food. She opens the door to a kitchen cuisine store. As the red door opens she sees the figure of a portly denim-clad white man with his back to her. When he turns to face her, the Frugal Gourmet holds out his hand and, taking her claw, pulls her to the window of the little shop.*

He points outside to Pimatisewin *and says to her in Cree, "She needs some tiramisu."*

---

* Dream.

† Life. Shorthand. Tree of Life.

B ERNICE OWNS TWO PAIRS OF SHOES. She thinks you
can tell a lot about someone by the shoes she wears. She
owns a pair of sneakers for work and a pair of five-inch heels
she found at a Sally Ann. Both serve a purpose. Neither, she
thinks, tells you anything about her except how she spends
her time. You can tell a lot about *most* people by their shoes,
she thinks.

How she spends her time is more and more often a mystery
to her. Hours seem to slip away without her noticing. Once
in a while, Bernice will find herself sitting so still and quiet
that she might be asleep. She is not, though. While she is not
entirely sure what she is doing, she is quite sure of what she
is not doing. And. Sleeping. Is not on the list.

When she first started to feel that something was happening, it was her body that informed her, and not her mind.
Sometimes, she would become aware that her legs were
cramping. From sitting in one place or position for too long.
Or. Maybe. From the control it took not to be where she was.
She couldn't tell. The odd time, it happened when someone
was around. During those moments she was not aware of
what she was doing but was almost always aware of "coming
back." When she did. Back when she did come back. Inevitably, someone without patience or kindness would be snapping their fingers at her, pushing at her with their foot, or, on
one occasion, yelling at her. ("Hey you fucking dummy, I am
talking to you!")

Sometimes, she would sit (she presumes motionless) for so
long in the cold or wind that her scars felt papery with the
cold air and her eyes were dry.

Back when she did come back, she would sit in the park, watching the fishing boats come in and the wind whip up the water. Moving and immobile at the same time, she had been content to just sit, watch and stare herself into her time. She would not try this at home. Would never have done so in Edmonton. But Gibsons is just safe. Enough.

Many people, she thinks, might have found this . . . this vacancy of her self − confusing or terrifying. Bernice didn't. That vacancy she felt was somehow absorbing; it sopped up everything around her, making her lighter. Lying in her bed, now, she thinks of that period as the time when she learned to leave. It became part of her, a continuum of change, growing in her until she could fully move and bend. Memories. Bad thoughts. Time. It felt like a rock skipping on water, so much so that she strangely is not shocked when she sinks. She has been strange for so long that she cannot even attempt to understand what normal might feel like. For her, coming back into her self after her time felt precisely normal. She may have felt this, but when she found cuts on her feet or bruises on her hands after one of these spells, or when she remembers the one time she came back with blood in and on her mouth and no cut, she did wonder where she had been. On that day, the last day of the boats on the water, she looked down and saw a note in her scarred and cut scabby hand:

muskeg
grapefruit
lemon
cumin

It is not her writing. It never is. She doesn't recognize her own handwriting anymore, though. It would have been hard to write through the bandages she had on her fingers anyway. In the time before she sank, her skin became mottled with some sort of fungus. Then, it looked scabby and raw. Now, in the light of her bedroom, it looks a bit like the blister rust that clings to the side of the lodgepole (pine) trees back home. When it first showed up, she would meticulously pick and scrape the rough scaly skin off what was first only her elbows, but which has now become attached to her calves, knees, hips, left thigh and, most recently, her fingers. The skin, which she peeled and let thicken, looks nothing like new skin from a fresh cut now. It resembles a peeled section of grapefruit, with the layering of tissue organized and neat. As the blisters spread she feels, instead of alienated from her skin, more at home in it. Like it is starting to look like she feels inside of it.

The more she scratched at it, the more it seemed to spread. She didn't mind, though, she thinks of herself as habitable. Desirable by something. More importantly, she thinks that she is somehow becoming. Something. Else.

It was hard to hide her hands from Lola and she feels relief now that no one pays attention to such things as sores. Back before – before she changed? Lay down? Sank? Before now, each day when she went in to work she would tape her fingers, wear long-sleeved shirts, favour the side of her neck without the creeping growth and hope that Lola would not notice. Bernice doesn't like conflict and Lola most certainly would have expressed her disapproval of her brown and angry red hands touching pastries, cake dough and mixing bowls if

Tracey Lindberg

she'd got a look at it. Lola has an opinion about everything and she most certainly would not have hesitated to make hers known. Bernice shudders – to an outsider it would look like a little tremor – to think what would happen if Lola found out that she ended up in Gibsons because of *The Beachcombers*.

She's not sure when it started, this – well, she hates to say, obsession. Somewhere along the way (before the Academy, before the Ingelsons, before Edmonton and before Gibsons), though, she seemed to have become preoccupied with these, these thoughts about Pat John. She didn't think it was out of control or anything. She just thinks he seems like a really nice guy. Like, getting his family parts on *The Beachcombers* whenever there was a need for more Indians.

Like everyone else, she watched his skinny arms in a cut-off T-shirt when the show came on in the early seventies. She waited for him to fall in love, but he never really did. And yes, she even followed him in the eighties when he seemed to be living on a diet of starch and sugar. But her love for Pat John flourished when he was playing young Jesse. Twenty years older than her, but still achievable: a healthy, working Indian man.

Anyhow, that's how she got here, to Gibsons, B.C. Well, actually, she got here via her friend Lettie from Sechelt. Lettie's old man was in the San at the same time as Bernice. They offered her some smoked salmon at lunch in the minty green hospital cafeteria, and while she never talked to them, just listened, Bernice found out they lived in Sechelt. So, once released and it became clear what she had to do, it seemed natural that she should show up on their doorstep. If Lettie thought it odd that a big Cree woman who had never spoken to her and who was institutionalized with her husband a year earlier should show up on her doorstep, she never let on. She (her old man was off fishing) let Bernice in, fed her some fish and bannock and was happy to have someone to talk to. Bernice took care of the kids while Lettie went shopping, cleaned the house and cooked. Even in her silence, even as she learned to absent her body, she kept Lettie company. One time Lettie took her and the kids to the Sechelt inlet, and while the kids ran around playing Bernice took in the water, the mountains and the air. The air smelled so clean. She had forgotten the smell of air, water, animal and life.

Lettie's people lived in four little villages, not really like a rez at all. Many of the men worked in fishing and fisheries and some of the women, like Lettie, worked in town. While she liked staying with Lettie and while the kids really latched on to her, Bernice wanted some quiet once in a while. It was a bit of a relief when Lettie's old man came home. Bernice took that to mean it was her time to go. She didn't feel too comfortable under the same roof as him, anyhow, so the next day she went into Gibsons to look for a job. From a Help Wanted sign set in an immaculate-looking window with precise letters that read "Lola's Little Slice of Heaven" Bernice found herself both a job and a home. After requiring her to make biscuits from scratch, Lola hired Bernice and offered her the apartment above the shop as well. It didn't seem to bother her that Bernice didn't do more than nod or slowly smile during the interview; in fact, she probably hadn't noticed. Lola, as it turned out, was a chatterer. As a result, Bernice

Tracey Lindberg

moved into the apartment above the restaurant (moved in: the Aer Lingus bag, a poster tube and a scabby old suitcase that brought to mind couches that you find on the street). It has been precisely three months since she left the San. Three months since she has been on the road. Three months since she had the dream.

The dream. In the dream, Jesse, Pat John, carved a ring from a tree and asked her to live with him. She left the hospital the morning after she had the dream. And, since Gibsons housed the actual Molly's Reach where TV Jesse worked — there she was.

She knows she is lucky to get this job, especially since Lola's Little Slice of Heaven did not include much interaction with, as Lola called all people with her own lack of pigmentation, "brownies." It wasn't so bad. Although, Bernice did have to shame her into changing the name of her "Happy Squaw Squares!" to brown sugar kisses. And Lola was not, well actually she was, as bad as you might think. But Bernice thinks that Lola has a really big heart and a head for numbers. You have to admire those parts of her even if you wouldn't invite her over for dinner, she supposes. She'd run into Lolas before in her life. Sure, her name was different and sometimes she was even a he, but it was the same person. Lolas were almost always fascinated because they had never met an Indian before.

I wonder how fascinated she'd be if she knew that I'd been fucked before I was eleven, Bernice thinks. *That I smoked pot every day; that I have read every Jackie Collins novel ever written — even the bad ones. Nope, that dying savage thing is what floats her boat.*

Lola had even called her "stoic" one day. That time, Bernice laughed and smiled and spat in the old bird's coffee when she turned to answer the phone.

So, her brief stay at the bakery has not been without friction. But, the thing that she keeps reminding herself of is that she came here with a goal in mind and that someday all of this sacrifice will be worth it. Sometimes she imagines it – Jesse walking in for some mocha cheesecake or for a snack. Later, she corrects the thought – just because he worked in Gibsons does not mean that he lives there.

Maybe, though, he will come back and visit, she thinks.

Anyhow, most often she pictures him alone, travelling in a jeep, stopping in at Starbucks (which would have to replace Ben's Bean There, Done That coffee shop) across the street. He'd be just about to hop in the jeep and then something would cause him to look into Lola's. He'd walk over, with that look he had when he decided to leave Molly's Reach that time. Serious and driven, the look told Bernice. He would walk into Lola's serious and driven.

Perplexed and torn (which is almost as good as serious and driven), he'd saunter, coffee in hand, into the restaurant. He was never actually perplexed or torn on *The Beachcombers*, but he was a real person after all. She always stopped on this part because she cannot drum up feelings for whomever Pat John looks like now. She is the same age he was when he took the role on the show. That would make him forty-five or fifty now, at least.

She has never told anyone about Jesse. Sure, family figured it out – what with her precisely scheduled TV shows and with the pictures she kept. But no one outside of the house

Tracey Lindberg

knew about her Jesse love. Especially not those guys she dated from home. Sometimes, if the guy had long hair, she pressed her lashes close together and looked at him through the lashed slits and he would almost look a bit like Jesse in the episode where he had two full lines to speak. Two verbs and even an adverb.

Nobody in Gibsons looks like Jesse. Everyone in Gibsons is very tanned – much darker than Bernice. And they also have good teeth. Lola told her there is fluoride in the water at Gibsons and that they probably didn't have it up north. Bernice keeps meaning to ask someone about that, but she can't do it. She doesn't want Auntie Val to worry – she was pretty freaked out when Bernice left. When she decided to go, she just took down her ancient pictures of Jesse (stolen from the Edmonton CBC office door) which she had since she was eleven, packed up a few things and was gone.

Thinking about the way she felt, about packing to move to be near Pat John, she feels a little silly. After all, he is likely an old man now. If she were to open her eyes, she knows she would see his picture from where she lies on her bed. It now hangs on what were the bare walls of the little studio above the bakery.

When she got there the place was sorely in need of some decorating. She didn't put up her pictures right away – she kept trying to figure out if the posters were the problem or if the posters came after the problem. Ordering seemed difficult, and she could not decide if her mind was skipping ahead to another time when she didn't want the posters up or if they needed to be there, like a reference book.

There's one that she knew she won't put up, that she never put up, of Jesse in a 1983 episode, the one where he punched a wall because he was so angry with Relic. She remembers that episode, that whole season, really clearly because that was the year that the show started coming on a half-hour later. She was still going to her uncle's even though her mom had quit macramé. Now instead, every Sunday, her mom and Auntie Maisie drove to bingo while uncle Larry watched her alone. Her mom and auntie were both on a losing streak that year. All that remained of the macramé class was nubby wall hangings, nubby plant hangers and nubby placemats. Her dad had taken off by then and she spent a lot of time thinking about the Cunninghams, Partridges and Bradys. Their white skin, white teeth and white walls without flaws.

It was that year that her uncle Larry started pressuring her to do more than sit on his lap and let him feel her up. So, she was still trying to figure out if those pictures of Jesse were up because of her uncle or if they were up despite him. Or to make something strange normal. Bernice didn't think so; she knows there was nothing normal about it, about him.

About Them.

A little breath, like a baby dreaming, escapes her. She imagines it landing on the floor beside the bed with a heavy thud.

One time when Maggie came to pick her up after bingo, it was winter, she thinks, Maggie looked at Bernice and asked if she was okay. Bernice wouldn't talk to her the whole way home. She wouldn't go to her uncle's house after that, no matter how hard her mom tried to get her to go. For a little while she stayed with their neighbours, Mr. and Mrs. Olson. Mr. Olson peed in a bag so he was okay. Eventually, her mom had to quit bingo and everything. Larry's wife, her Auntie Maisie, came to talk to her one time after that. She brought her a *Tiger Beat* magazine with a fold-out poster of Fonzie and it was stuffed in a gift-sized Canada Post mailbox. They must have been on sale after Christmas from the post office. When she found that there was a lock and a key for the mailbox, Bernice threw the whole thing on the floor of her room, enraged at her auntie's seeming complicity in Larry's secret-making.

She had that mailbox with her for years, in the top corner of her closet. It was heavy and metal – if there was one made now it would be made of plastic. Bernice eventually got it down and used it for locking up her journal, wearing the key around her neck. Eventually she outgrew it.

I've got bigger secrets now, I guess, she thinks.

Sometimes she gets mad when she thinks about that: his wife giving her a gift for secrets. Then she sometimes thinks that she should cut her some slack. There was no way, Bernice thinks, that any woman could live knowing that sort of thing and do nothing. She may have almost given up on men but she still holds a quiet place in her head for women.

Every once in a while when she was working at Lola's she thought about what would have happened if she'd known how to use butcher knives back then. She put that out of her head, she had to or her hands started shaking and she had to take a pull off her inhaler. Whatever those were, they usually passed pretty quick, though.

Well, usually.

She goes upstairs, heart pounding. Her head is cottony and

her chest is too full. She tries to think of three things like they taught her in the San. Three things to calm her down. One thing she hears. The hum of the air conditioner cooling the room from the heated ovens. One thing she sees. The poster tube on the top shelf of her closet. One thing she feels. The butcher's knife under the mattress leaving a small lump near where she sits. She does not calm down.

2

AT HOME

witokemakan: one who lives with the family

pawatamowin
She feels a caress on her cheek, a cool hand on her warm brow, and hears the gentle hoot hoot hoot of kohkohkohow.* *She dreams: "Ah, so it's night, after all." Looking into the sleepmirror she sees talon scratches on her face.*

---

* A small owl.

T HE DREAM OF THE OWL comes back four nights in a row. When she surfaces on the fourth morning she feels in love. Like she fell in love during the night. She can feel arms around her and thinks maybe she forgot a dream about Jesse. It feels different though – and she has had many a dream where she woke up in love with him. This warmth feels like she thinks home would feel like. Well, someone's home, anyways.

She remembers her mom best in the kitchen. Light feet, thick sauces and silences. Heavy sighs. It is hard to imagine Maggie as a girl going to prom in the too-big hand-me-down dress. ("That dress is too old for you," her date had said. Admiringly and accusingly.) She is petite, bird-like, her small bones placed delicately in her daughter and hidden, early, under layer after layer of fat. Her tininess always undermined by the space she took up in the room. Or rather, by the space her spirit took up in the room. She was seemingly exhausted by the mere effort of being alive. Throw some kids, nieces, nephews and a daughter into the mix, and no matter how kind and how pure her love, they all feel the burden. Of being in the way.

The area she takes is notional, but Bernice was always aware when she had crossed into a space coveted by Maggie. A purse filled with old chocolate bar wrappers, the candy never having made it into the home. Or worse. Nibbled when no one was around. Bernice always felt this was a betrayal, the hoarding of treats that she would never see. Never taste. It seemed to her to be unsound mothering, the keeping of a secret.

Other secrets crawled out from under dark spaces. In arguments peppered with profanity, shooting like buckshot at the unfortunate man/men drinking nearby, Maggie yelling that she couldn't stand being around all of "those damn kids." Like Bernice hadn't come from her body. As if Maggie's nieces and nephews weren't of her blood. Weren't her responsibility. *Thosing* a wedge in between them. Or, during drunken reminiscences where her mom told her that if she had only married her teenage boyfriend (was it the one who thought her prom dress too mature? Bernice wondered) she would be a little Spanish baby. "But, I wouldn't be *me* then, Mom, would I?" she had asked a silently brooding Maggie.

All of it added to a knowledge, lodged as deep as those chocolate bar wrappers in a purse, that Maggie would rather an Other. Another. Another life. With fewer nieces, nephews and Bernices around. Kids who weren't so noisy. A kid who she wouldn't catch gulping mashed potatoes by the handful in the kitchen after dinner one night so that she couldn't fit hand-me-down clothes and had to have new clothes every time she gained weight. Which was often.

Maybe if she had an Other, Bernice wouldn't have found her lying on her back in bed every night, staring at the ceiling as if she could not see it, possibly dreaming of the life she would have had. In her mind's eye, Bernice remembers important moments like snapshots that she has taken. Luckily, she can bring up the images anytime she wants. Since she sank, she flows through past and present easily, like water flows through a drainpipe. Time became fluid in the days in between Edmonton and Gibsons. She doesn't have recall – not the way she can look back at her time at Little Loon. Different than thinking about living at the San. This is something else. Time does flow, but it is not with the rush of a river. It trickles like a stream that Bernice can float down, paddle back in, and start over at a new current. In a way, Gibsons was a tributary branching off the crashing flow of her past. She drifts lazily, some eddy pulling her. She arrived in Gibsons on a gentle tributary off the roar of the river that carried her from Loon to B.C. Was pushed to Lola's. Paddled in place until Freda roared up and started keeping vigil at her side in the little bakery apartment. Felt her cousin next to her, solid in her small bones, the curve of her back next to her on the bed, trying to anchor her. Bernice lies in bed, motionless, but feels the gentle rush of water against her as she makes her way upstream. Past her past. It feels peaceful. She knows she will have to push her way upstream sometime. For now, she floats, feeling anything but free. For now, she knows it is enough to be able to slip along without plunging. For now, she stays in bed, none of the women-gathering around her aware that she is travelling. Bernice knows, somewhere at the core of her, that she is on a voyage. Whether it is to someplace or from it, she is not sure. All she knows is that water is woman. Protective. She does not fear sinking. Not because it cannot happen, but because she prefers it to open terrain. Lola noticed, of course. She must have called Freda. Freda, who never panicked, must have called Auntie Val. And now, all three of them take turns sitting on, standing by, waiting on the mattress. Taking to her bed ("Her sickbed") was as easy as, or even easier than, breathing. Her un/conscious decision was one her spirit made. When it was time, and when the fury of her past began to race ahead of her future, she simply lay down.

Tracey Lindberg

From her bed, she sometimes imagines her mom into the old pictures she has seen of Indian women in historical books and anthropological texts. She can see her there easily – dark, unsmiling and with two black braids, long and thick and hanging down her back. She had pure brown chocolatey skin, not mocha latte like Bernice's own. She would have, always in motion, stopped only for the moment it took to snap the photo: a tiny whirlwind on chromatic tape.

Sometimes Bernice can see Maggie's bones when she looks in the mirror. Most usually, though, they are like fishbones; you don't see them but you know they are there. With those bones buried deep within her, Bernice knows she has protection that no one knows about.

She is not like her cousins or her aunties who wear their bones like armour. Cousin Freda's bones stick out every which way. She looks like someone's idea of an Indian. Like a warrior. Cheekbones, hipbones, collarbones jutting out in warning. It seems to her that Freda's little bones are angry. Notice me! Notice me! Notice me!

Bernice and her Auntie Val are not the type they took pictures of – the type they remembered and wanted to remember. No one likes the fat Indian women. Well, the men sure did, but no one wants to put them on postcards and imprints to send back home. Maybe fat was not noble enough. In a way it has always made Bernice proud. She and her auntie, much like the pioneers who had to "break their land alone," she thinks, and covers her mouth to stifle a laugh which could alert Freda and Lola downstairs to her presence in her body.

Those images run through her mind. While outwardly still, inside, Bernice's mind is churning, alive. A charged battery in a resting machine, only her body idles in wait. For a sign. For completion. For the moment. When she is safest. Pictures swim together with memories like a slide show. Val and Freda active, her diminutive mom passive and almost out of frame. One shot, of her father, walking away. Remembering them, re-remembering them, she wanders around the borders of her emotional ground zero, never quite approaching and never quite looking directly at it, hoping to find survivors of the place she ran away from.

Another image. One hot Alberta summer when her mom and her Auntie Val were in their cups, she heard them become loud louder loudest after a night of drinking. She didn't really understand the link between the booze and the joy that was coming from the kitchen and pictured the two sisters sitting close and laughing like best friends over their near-empty glasses. The Canadian Club bottle, she had imagined, would be sitting between them as they by turns laughed and swung their long black hair over their shoulders, and curled over in their chairs with laughter.

They were so pure in their appreciation of and love for one another that she felt lightheaded. That night, she had thought about waking Freda up to see this joy, but that girl slept like her conscience was clear. Which it shouldn't be, Bernice reminds herself.

Listening to the sounds from the kitchen, she had imagined them braiding each other's hair and whispering secrets to one another whenever the room got silent. She pressed her ear to the wall separating the kitchen from her tiny bedroom and heard:

Her auntie saying, with pure emotion, "Sister, promise me when I get old that you will pluck my chin."

Maggie responding, with all of the seriousness of a bride at the altar, "I will, sister. I will."

From this evening, she learned two things. First, she was likely to have a facial hair problem when she grew up. It was okay, she had a sister (well, Skinny Freda anyhow) too. Also, she would have to learn to do anything for one other person in her life. She would find a person with whom she could exchange a solemn vow when they were in their cups. And they too would be alive in her memory.

The creaking from another kitchen and the bakery heat rising give her pause from her memory travelling for a moment. She is taking stock. It is less an inventory than a patchwork quilt. No matter where she starts, body still and mind moving, emotions on high alert, she ends up at Loon. Freda's wild laugh makes its way up the stairs, landing on her comforter expectantly. Bernice does not move, does not want to feel it. Will not welcome it under the covers. She remembers that laughter.

❧

The roar of the powerboats is alive in her mind. Water. Sunshine. Auntie Val. Freda. In her mind's eye she sees pictures change and exchange. They pull her attention to the water. She can see the engine churning up an angry lather which a pink man jumped over with either fearless agility or reckless disregard. A girl in a multicoloured near-bikini cheered him on – a flash of white teeth, white hair and brown skin, browner than Bernice's own. The skier fell with a spectacular splash, his body stopped fully and quickly as he snowplowed under a crest. She remembers that day.

"Leggo've the rope," Auntie Val, Skinny Freda and Bernice yelled in unison.

Bernice peeled an orange and telekinetically willed the blond bikini woman from the seat where she sat perched, healthy and mane tossing, into the churning wake behind the outboard.

"Too bad about Willie Belcourt, eh?" Skinny Freda said to them, leaving the blond bikini momentarily safe from Bernice's ire.

"Eh?" Auntie Val cocked an eyebrow. While Skinny Freda was actually her niece, Skinny Freda was also Valene's best friend and adopted daughter and was well known never to let the truth get in the way of a good story. Val offered her a cookie and motioned for Skinny Freda to go on. Bernice remembers with particular delighthorror the silver sparkly two-piece bathing suit that her auntie wore with the pride and assurance of someone wearing a buffalo robe.

Bernice ignored the cookie and closed her eyes to the sun. She had lost seven pounds, most of it from her legs, and had daringly worn shorts that day. She had been at Loon for a month and did not have to go back to Christ's Academy for six more weeks. That is, if they found the money for another school year. She hoped that her weight loss and tanned legs would keep the other fourteen-year-old girls at bay.

"Well," Skinny Freda started, with a Storyteller's expertise, "he took off to St. Albert with that white woman, you know." Freda said it all with a natural lilt and no judgment. She herself had dated a few *moniawak** since Val started letting her date. Bernice looked at her sideways; her sistercousin seemed an inverted version of herself. Bernice had always thought that Freda's confidence flowed out from under shadowed crevasses and angled bones. That some mélange of svelte certitude, magazine model skinnyhappiness leeched out of her in places where silence and stuffing found Bernice wanting. It would be years before she understood that the funhouse mirror of their shared childhood would alter the ways they saw themselves and warp what others saw in them.

"Freddy, just tell the story." Bernice said it with more impatience than she felt. She remembers that her auntie looked at her from the corner of her eye, wondering about her agitation, she imagined.

"Anyways," Skinny Freda said, deliberately slow, "he leaves Flora behind, just like every year, only this year his trapline has that white woman on it."

She looked at Valene and then Bernice expectantly.

Auntie Val, clearly interested, pretends not to be. Freda could be antagonistic, the kind of person who left bannock on her plate, knowing you wanted it, and not offering it until you were about to walk away. It's a style of Cree passive aggressiveness Bernice has come to know well. Val, used to this, feigned lack of interest. "And . . ." she begrudgingly nudged.

"And, when he comes back from St. Albert to rest with

---

* White men. White people.

Flora for the winter, she has got a great big white guy living with her!"

Auntie Val was ecstatic. "Flora? She never fools around!"

Skinny Freda's enthusiasm escalated. "And, he is living on the reserve with her."

"No!" Valene and Bernice echoed each other.

"And . . ."

"Don't say it! Don't say it! She's . . ." Valene was flailing with her own bigelegance and people on the beach were staring.

". . . having his baby!" Skinny Freda finished triumphantly, taking Val's cigarette and flicking two inches' worth of ashes to the sand, enjoying the laughter bubbling from Val's substantial belly.

"True?" Bernice asked.

"Yeah. She met him at that benefit at Loon, you know, the environmentalists put it on. The *Pimatisewin*," Skinny Freda added, as if more details made it more believable.

Sated, they sat in silence for a while pondering good love gone bad. After a bit, Auntie Val and Skinny Freda traded stories about other romances. If they noticed Bernice's silence, they ignored it and let her be.

She thought about the *Pimatisewin* and the benefit and wondered whether that old tree would make it. There were supposed to be four of them, two in North America and two in South America. The one at Loon Lake was in sad shape. She had heard the one in B.C. was dying too, from pollution, they said. Chief and Council and the whole community had joined together to try and save it. She hoped they would spend the benefit money on something that would make the tree better.

She grabbed a Coke, opened it and passed it to her auntie. When she was done, Valene offered it to Skinny Freda, who shook her head and passed it to Bernice. She was just about to decline when a pale towheaded boy from a pack of teenagers yelled out to her, "Hey, you think you need that?"

Skinny Freda had sprung up from the blanket and started walking towards the group.

"Fuck you!" Skinny Freda yelled at him, startling her friends as much as the youths, who were still young enough to be frightened by the authority or unpredictability of adults.

"Such a lady," Bernice said with some degree of awe.

"Don't give respect and you don't get it," Auntie Val pronounced like she said it herself. She was proud of her daughterniece's spirit.

They packed up their belongings and headed for Skinny Freda's truck, leaving posturing and bewildered boys in the wake of their grandeur.

∾

There is something about that summer, something stuck in her that she can't quite figure out. Like a hint or a whisper, it gently sits in her mind while she steeps in her own disquiet on her mattress. The feeling that joins her in the still room is one of almost longing. Near aching. She becomes aware of her physical self because the emotions pain her.

She notices that Freda keeps coming up and was talking more and more today, but she doesn't feel like listening. Maybe, she thought, it was because of the Frugal Gourmet.

This morning he made "Pine Nut Pastry." The last time she had pastry was at her uncle's wake. Even though Lola had plenty of pastry around, Bernice has not been able to eat it since she got to Gibsons. Or, since the wake for that matter. Food could take you back, she thinks.

Food no longer seems to be a problem for her. In fact, in her sleepingwake state, she has no desire for food. What she craves is alone, like a dry drunk craves a drink. The appetite she has is for the shift, and until that is met, she is pretty certain she will not need any more food. And, while she still cannot seem to eat anything, she is sleeping better.

acimowin*

This is a good story; it makes all the young girls laugh.
There was a speck of dust that was always
getting in everyone's way.
Then one day, the dust, she flew
into the wrong man's eye.
"Ayuh," he said to that dust.
"You are always bodderin' me and now I will send you
Away."
And with one wave, he turned
That dust into an Owl.
Next day, that owl, she comes back and
She flies right to his face
And pecks his eye out.
That's why the girls always catches
the boys' eyes.

* Story.

3

BERNICE TRAVELS LIGHTLY

awasispihk: before. the time before

pawatamowin

She is walking to the Pimatisewin *with Auntie Val and Skinny Freda. In the dream, it's in sad shape. Indian summer only and the leaves are gone and the branches reach out in need. There are some old people who came from all over, standing, kneeling, sitting and praying around the tree. As she approaches, she notices a little woman stirring a pot over a fire near the base of* Pimatisewin. *The woman shakes her head and her kerchief falls off to reveal the wizened old face of her employer Lola. Lola whispers to the women that there is no more food for the tree. She tells them that the old tree is a* Kohkom* *tree and continues to stir her pot.*

* Grandmother.

WHEN BERNICE SURFACES, the air feels different, and the smell in the restaurant below is sweet and almost cloying. As she hasn't seen Lola today, she assumes her employer is having a dessert special and that she wants to pay attention to the food. It is not that Lola is a bad cook – she is a great cook – but in truth she is an average baker. She had relied on Bernice for her good baking sense. Bernice somewhat petulantly wonders how the baked goods are faring without her to cook them, but thinks better of it and goes back to sleep.

She wakes at 4:00 and can tell that neither Lola nor Skinny Freda is there. She deliberates whether she should turn on the TV at 5:00, but decides that she had better not. If she moves too much, she knows, people will start to ignore her. Freda would be especially vigilant in her disregard – her inattention in a crisis is legendary.

When her dinner was not delivered, she knew that there was something going on in the restaurant. Hearing laughter outside and the screams of unbridled exuberance, Bernice wonders if it is a holiday. It is hard to tell, because the Frugal Gourmet does not do themes and is in perpetual reruns, but the sky looked bright and was losing that tint, like a frosted amber, that it got when the air was cold.

Back home, spring was richer and more generous than on the coast. You could feel the crack of a different ice under your foot and know that there was no more snow coming. A certain rabbit made a quick appearance and you knew that it would not get cold again.

You could also tell when it was spring because you got your first near-glimpse of Freda's boobs, she thinks, biting her lips to keep from smiling. While it was certainly true that spring heralded higher heels, shorter skirts and deeper necklines for her cousin, it was not nice to reflect upon it in that way. Or to think that a glimpse of Freda's ass was perhaps a little more frequent than a spring groundhog, but just about as accurate.

The two of them could not be less similar. There is, Bernice knows, a strength in each of them. There is also an unforgiving nature that each of them possesses that is completely unlike the makeup of Val or her mom. However, if there was one thing that all four women shared, it was their absolute reliance on only themselves. Having seen all of their fathers and husbands walk out the door (with booze or a brunette in hand), each woman understood most completely the nature of women's interconnectedness. Being reliant upon only women also had meant that the particulars of problem solving were addressed in ways known to women and using women's methods. So, while Freda might be from the school of dirty lickins' field of thought, all four of the women had always maintained graceful coherence for the sake of the family and the community. A grotty one, but still a coherence. There was some sort of over-responsibility that weighed on each one of them, as if carrying the load that the men had dropped cost them posture and emotional affluence that could not yet be counted.

Bernice wonders how far back, how many generations ago, it was that women took on children, family, home and provisioning. In her community, the men went away. Some to the cities. To work. Or not. Some to prison. Rightfully or not. Some just went away and you wouldn't hear a word about them for years.

Bernice sometimes thinks this was for the best. When her dad left, she did not think (at the time) that it was for the best. She feels a pain in her throat whenever she thinks about her dad. It is nothing like the pain in her chest that she gets when she thinks about her mother. It is like the difference between a penny dropped in a puddle and a riptide.

⌘

"Put that down, girl, you know that after five o'clock it's mix, not pop," her uncle Louis had barked at her.

She'd jumped a little and all of the adults, some of them louder than others, laughed as Bernice put the Coke bottle down. If she drank a glass of it, it would mean that someone might have to leave the house later in the evening to pick up another bottle. She knew it would be all right to make a smart remark and then pour herself a glass. As long as she made them laugh she would be forgiven. She didn't want the Coke that badly though.

Her uncle had snorted at her meanly, "Lose some weight."

She had walked out of the room to her mother's voice. "Really, Lou, one glass isn't going to be missed," her mom said.

"That kid's too sensitive," she heard her uncle mutter.

She was sorry to have left her room. She looked at the pile of library books on her floor (the carpet was the kind that is supposed to feel like grass when it's green) and felt better. Back then, Saturday was just about her favourite day of all. She would spend about four hours in the town library, about three and a half hours too many by Miss Robbins' watch. Miss Robbins, Bernice imagined, was at least seventy years old. She was almost certain that Miss Robbins, Clara Robbins, was a smoker. She had arthritic fingers and knew every title on the shelves of the Grande Prairie public library. The skin on her fingers, spotted, yellow and papery thin, would tap past books at an alarming rate as she tried to select what Bernice could read. She also remembered the old woman, wearing orange lipstick that was an orange not found in nature, as being mistrustful.

"Bernice Meetoos, I think that book is too old for you. Judy Blume is not for ten-year-olds," she said slyly one time, not at all in a librarian voice, but in what Bernice thought was an in-sin-u-ating voice. She was not quite sure what that meant, but she thought it had something to do with putting sin into someone else. She had read it in the *New Yorker* (which caused Miss Robbins to smack her lips against her teeth louder than ever before). She had presumed this was because Miss Robbins was prone to put sin into whatever motives a ten-year-old girl might have.

Bernice's momma had a standing policy that Bernice could read whatever she wanted. Well, she could at least bring home whatever she wanted. Bernice assumed this was because her mom was the best judge, after Bernice of course, of what Bernice should have been reading. Bernice reminded Miss Robbins of this for the sixteen thousandth time.

Miss Clara Robbins clucked her tongue on the roof of her

Tracey Lindberg

mouth and said, "I'd certainly like to meet this mother of yours."

To Bernice it sounded like she didn't believe that Bernice had a mother.

She stuck out her tongue at Miss Robbins as she swung her wide librarian bottom around and, while fascinated by the girth of the bottom, continued her search for the perfect book.

The perfect book, to Bernice, would depict a clean house with flowers in every available container. There would be no cigarette burns in gaudy-coloured carpet, no empty bottles or glasses half-drunk or spilled on the floor on weekends, and no visits without invitations from her parents' friends. No one would bother her in her room under the stairs, and she wouldn't be woken up by thundering feet up the steps (a fight) or the thudding down the stairs (someone falling down). There would be happy shiny people who always hugged and smiled. They would never put each other down or make fun of one another to make other people laugh.

They would take family vacations to Disneyland, go for walks as a family, and sit down for meals and ask each other questions they had always wanted to know the answers to. There would be another daughter who was a little chubby, popular and smart. The other daughter, who was, coincidentally, the same age as Bernice, would wear store-bought clothes, have her hair cut in parlours (Bernice loved that word; she also loved "turgid," "nomenclature" and "conglomerate"), and would not have to take out books from the library because she would have her own library. She might let close friends borrow her books, but certainly would never let strangers, and definitely never lend her favourites. She could read books to her heart's content, never having to stop for macramé lessons, visits from relatives, or to wonder what was going on above her head when someone crashed or fell down the stairs.

She never found the perfect book and contented herself with stories about families that sounded perfect.

The sound of raucous (she thought it came from "ruckus") laughter raced through the living room to the storage room (and now her bedroom) under the stairs. She tapped the door quietly with her toe (which she could do from the bed, having perfected this move years ago) to close it, not wanting to be noticed. She thought better of it and opened it again and slammed it a little, just enough so they'd be aware that she had closed the door. She could see the last of the winter daylight coming under it, just a crack and a reminder that the perfect families did not have to slam doors to tell people to go home.

Then came the sound of female blurry laughter that followed the slamming of her door.

"You made yer point, kiddo," her mom's friend Terry yelled in after her. Bernice's mom thought Terry was her friend, but Bernice knew a secret. Terry really liked her dad. One night when she got up to get a glass of water she saw Terry rubbing up against her dad in the kitchen. She noticed that her dad's breathing was funny. From this, she took it that her dad did not seem to mind it so much. She sat down on a chair stubbornly and waited until they saw her. Terry smiled and rushed over. "What's the matter, sweetie? Did you have a bad dream?" She bent over Bernice and brushed her hair out of her eyes.

Bernice felt woozy from the smell of smoke and wine on Terry's breath. She looked at her dad and said deliberately to Terry, "Your shirt's undone."

She got up and went to her room, leaving Terry to jerkily arrange herself to her father's laughter.

"Little brat," she heard her say to her dad through the door, which she had her ear pressed to.

"She's a smart little 'breed, that one," she heard him say proudly, and though she listened until, exhausted, she fell asleep, she couldn't hear any sounds from the kitchen.

She bristled at the word "'breed" (it would be years before she understood all the implications of being called a "Half-breed"). Or, maybe it was because she didn't want to associate it with the "most intimate of acts." Bernice had started reading a Harlequin Romance early in the summer, and that's what they called it. Her uncle Larry had forgone any notion of intimacy and called it "boning." She didn't like that word, either. It reminded her of de-boning and chickens. The image of fat and flesh grinding together and apart made her feel queasy. She had a really weak stomach and she had to be careful what she thought about or she would make herself throw up. It had gotten her out of school a few times until her momma got wise to her.

She didn't go to school so much, anyways. Sometimes her mother had one of her headaches and Bernice would walk around quietly until she got up. It was usually 11:00 or 12:00 by then and she would just read in bed until someone discovered her. Other times she would plead sickness and no one seemed too concerned. Bernice had missed more days than anyone else at school and she had still done fairly well on her report card. A few times she had actually been sick and her mother had comforted her and tried to make her as comfortable as possible by giving her a glass of ginger ale with the bubbles stirred out or tea with a lot of milk in it. One time, though, when she complained of a stomach ache, her mom put a little piece of soap up her bum. She thought long and hard about her ailments and excuses after that.

The front door opened, inviting the freezing air into the house, and she could feel it even in her room. The house got quiet soon after, and with the exception of her mother's burdened steps across the floor (a sound she knew was a part of the post-party cleanup) there was no other sound in the house. She felt herself relax a bit and did the deep breathing that her doctor told her to do when she thought she felt her asthma coming on. There was still too much smoke in the air and the deep breathing made her feel dizzier. Still, she liked the house better this way, with just her and her mother there alone. Freda was still out at *Kohkom*'s, she spent most of her time there now, and would not be home until Monday.

Her mom poked her head under the stairs, without knocking. "You want some Coke now, my girl?"

She followed her mom to the kitchen, remarkably clean again, and filled up a glass. They sat at the table, it was one of their rituals, and she watched as her momma rolled smokes. Sometimes at night she would wake up to the tap tap tapping of her mom as she made sure the tobacco fell all the way to the filter. Her mom would sit up, sometimes for hours, just smoking and staring at the kitchen wall. Her silence scared Bernice, who was dependent upon other people's noise to fill her own quiet.

Even through the smoke and beer fumes, her mom smelled of freshly baked bread and onions. It was a comforting smell, one of home, and it filled the room on days like today when her mom baked and froze bread, buns and bannock for the family.

"What are you doing, all holed up in there?" She pointed with her lips to Bernice's room and waited for her girl's response.

"Reading a new book."

"Already? Gosh, where are you gonna put all of those words, Birdie?"

Her mom looked at her then, serious and thoughtful. Bernice, used to shrinking from attention, looked away. "You know, you're gonna be the first one of us to go to school. I never have to worry about you, and I always know that no matter what happens, Bernice will be all right.

"You look so much like your auntie, you are so lucky you got the looks and the brains," her mom told her. "Good thing you didn't get her . . ." Maggie Meetoos paused. ". . . full nature." She laughed.

Bernice started and covered her mouth with her hand involuntarily. She didn't know that her mom thought she was pretty. She had always thought of Freda as the pretty one, the one who got attention. She also wondered what Auntie Val's full nature was. Something in her ears let her know that it was not necessarily a good thing.

"You know your auntie used to be a bookworm too?" her mom asked her.

Two secrets. Two things she did not know. It came to Bernice that her mom was drunk. Maggie kept secrets like some women kept canned goods: sealed and in the dark until they were needed. When her mom was drunk, Bernice tried to balance her fear with her fascination. And while it always scared her, her stomach knotting instantly and her back tense, it was a lot like sitting in the lodge: people were quite hard to make out but you couldn't wait for what you heard next. The problem was, though, that as her mom relaxed, Bernice got more and more tense. On those rare occasions, less rare as Bernice grew up, when her mother drank to excess, Bernice would hide in the basement and read under a shoulder-high lamp near the dryer. She turned the dryer on to generate heat and to block out the noise of the adults upstairs. White noise drowning out the brown noise.

"When you were a little girl, *iskwesis,*" her mother said, "your Auntie Valene hugged you to herself and told me that you were her daughter."

Maggie shifted awkwardly in her chair, as if the booze made her uncomfortable in her skin. "I'd never seen anyone so in love with another person that was not their birthchild."

To Bernice's amazement, her mom's eyes had filled up.

"She is your *kee kuh wee sis,* your little mother."

Three secrets. Three. She had another mom.

"When Val went . . ." – Maggie searched her daughter's face to see what the smart girl knew – ". . . away – away from here – she never called or nothing. Just left, mad at us and crazy at the world. When she came back, she wasn't the same anymore."

Noticing the worry on her daughter's face, she said, "She loves you just as much, Birdie, she's just lost the piece of her that knows how to show it."

Showing it is precisely the thing that Bernice struggles with as she remembers that moment. Inside her, she swells with memories and prickles with bodily reminders of her life. Before. Here. Her body and her emotions are inseparable now, her Sealy mattress a vessel within which one thing becomes indiscernible from another. Lying there, filled with a mix of emotions and feelings: hurt, pain, longing, love and remorse – Bernice's body reveals none of this in its calm. To Freda and Lola, whom she can feel the worry on like a hangover, she is failing, but she knows better. This is a gathering.

Her strength is surely being tested, she thinks. Her ache for home, home being something she does not yet under-stand, and a place she has never been, brushes over her like a skirt hem on the floor. If the women could see her insides, she imagines they would see a churning, a quickening, a real live storm inside of her. Whatever was happening, her pulse remains the same while her skin feels lit from within.

The feeling is a little bit like that moment before fainting, if she remembers correctly. She is a bit of an expert and remem-bers it felt like taking off and then putting on your skin again. She tries to think of herself as a moose stew. She will know when she is done. Her mom made the best moose stew; maybe it was because the meat was always fresh, maybe it was because her bannock was served with it, but that stew was like a tonic that could cure most things. Maybe, she thinks, moose is home.

The last time she had fresh moose was in the fall, before she moved into the city to go to school. She would have been twelve or thirteen. Her mom, of course, made it. Tiny and weary, her mom was unusually heavy on her feet as she got up and walked to the tall pine cupboard that she had recently painted and put in the kitchen. Her short brown arm barely touched the rear of the cupboard and she almost disappeared as she reached for something in the back. Bernice saw her eyes flutter as she grasped what she was looking for and tipped it with her fingers in to get it. She pulled out a brown box, which rattled with change. Her mom seemed to have trouble holding her balance, and she veered a bit towards the stairs trying to make it back to her chair at the table.

Her mom had fished out a five-dollar bill. "Can you go and get me some salt from the HiLo? It's still early and we're gonna need some tonight."

"Salt tonight? We still have lots." She had lifted the shaker, shaped like a fat dancing white woman. It felt heavy.

"Ayuh, we'll need more, I'm gonna dry some meat and make some stew tonight."

"Tonight?" She was trying to get her mom to talk because she didn't want to go outside in the dark and in the windy cold.

"Don't stall, put your clothes on. The sooner you get out there the sooner you will get home."

Bernice had trudged to the front door and put on her jacket.

"Not that one, the parka, and you'd better put your snow pants on, too."

"I'll look stupid, I hate those pants, Mom, they're too small and they make me look . . ." – she searched for a word – ". . . like a bimbo."

Bimbo the Birthday Clown was on every Saturday at 6:30

Tracey Lindberg

in the morning during the *Uncle Bobby* show. He was the worst part of the Professor Kitzel, Max the Mouse and Spider-Man marathon that she, Freda and whichever cousins were over used to watch together.

"Don't use that word in this house," her mother spat venomously at her. "Don't you ever use that word."

Though tiny, she solidly planted herself in front of Bernice, and assumed a threatening stance. For a second she was afraid her mom would smack her.

"Don't hit me." Bernice cowered in the corner, fully dressed and hopefully padded enough with her coat, snow pants and mitts not to feel the blow too hard.

Something had registered on her mom's face. Something at once shocked and ashamed. She stepped back and said quietly, "Get out, Birdie, go for a walk and get some air. You spend too much time indoors. Go now."

In the stillness of her room, Bernice hears her own breath, a bit ragged. She can feel her mom's resignation to something but doesn't want to know what it is. Above the rumble of the noise from the bakery, she barely registers and refuses to recognize something from her mother that is at once familiar and painful. Her palate for pain, though, is well developed. She recognizes the flavour in her mouth as bitter and dull. It tastes like defeat.

Bernice had put on a toque and stepped into the early evening dark of the near-winter. The wind wheezed and whistled at her as she trudged through the new snow. It was hard and starting to get packed beneath her feet, and she thought that it was starting to get that brown sugar feel. She walked as quickly as her asthma and padding would allow her. She crossed the main road only when all of the traffic had passed, and when she started to move again she felt a chill in her legs that served as notice that she had been standing on the roadside for a very long time.

She slipped and almost fell on the icy lot of the HiLo Mart.

"Nice move, buffalo," a voice called out.

It was Tim Lerat, dressed in a jean jacket and hunting cap. He looked even spookier at night with his hair unkempt and a cigarette dangling from his lips. He was, of course, with a group of younger boys who tried to look and act like him whenever possible.

"Yeah, way to go," echoed Shorty Moostoos. He was fifteen, two years younger than Tim, but he was just a bit taller than Bernice.

"Get bent," she yelled at them as she reached the door, silently thanking Mickey Spillane for the comeback.

She watched them warily through the glass of the HiLo, but only when she turned corners and stopped to stare at goods on the shelves. They were waiting for her like the wolves in *Call of the Wild.* She imagined them scratching at the glass, the hard nails of animals clicking against glass as they frantically tried to scratch through to their prey.

She looks at Old Man Pocock, he watched her every move, the owner of the HiLo trusted no one. But Bernice knew all about him. He suspected that everyone did what he had been doing for years, trying to make the best of his situation by ripping off the old, imbecilic and immature. Surrounded in his wealth, he wanted more and couldn't see what he had. He was

Tracey Lindberg

like the men in *The Little Prince* who could not see a single rose in their flower gardens because they were always looking for more. She was certain he saw only a hat, and smiled because she could not only see the elephant that lived within the snake, she could hear it call to her.

"What are you looking for, Bernice Meetoos?" He yelled at her from a table-length away.

She glanced at the door; the wolves were still there, spitting and smoking as all bad wolves do.

"I'm, uh, looking for, uh, some salt." She knew she was standing right in front of the boxed Sifto.

"Are you blind? It's right there." He lurched off his stool and pointed to, but did not touch, the salt. It was almost like he didn't want to touch something that she was about to buy and take home.

"Oh, thanks, yeah, I see it."

She lifted it off the shelf and dropped it immediately, the sound of Shorty's laughter as Tim howls startling her. She looked towards the door and sees that Tim had taken his pants off, no – had pulled them down, to reveal his bottom, cleaved, spread and pressed against the glass directly in front of her.

She stared at this display in wonder. She was quite sure he had hair on his bum.

She looked at Old Man Pocock and pretended she didn't see what he knew she saw. Walking to the till, she pulled off her mitten and took out the five-dollar bill. She passed it to him and watched him carefully as he counted out her change with the three fingers he had on his right hand. She waited for him to put the change on the counter, but as usual, he stood there until she put her hand out to receive the change. He has stopped trying to shortchange her as her math skills have caught him twice before. Freda told her that the old man does it for fun, to separate the smart kids from the dumb ones. Bernice didn't care and never lingered in the store.

"I'd like a bag, please."

He grunted and reached under the counter; he had never offered her a bag in her whole life.

She turned slowly on her heel and was relieved to find that the wolves had disappeared. She knew that they wouldn't be far away, though, and she ran the three blocks home. When she reached the corner of her street she was wheezing and puffing, her breath was shallow and it came from her throat. She slowed down and tried to do her deep-breathing exercises.

By the time she reached her house her breathing was almost normal. There were vehicles parked in the driveway and in front of the house. She walked to her uncle Larry's truck, as it seemed to be in the centre of the driveway. Sometimes he had cases of beer in the back of his truck. She thought that she would hide them if he did. She had done this before, and on two of the occasions the party broke up early. She looked in the window of his Chevy and saw Terry's purse spilled on the seat. She can tell that it was hers because the leather was bright green. It must have come from a cow something like the horses in *The Wizard of Oz* at the Emerald City, she thought.

She looked in the back of the truck and found not beer, but blood. It looked like a pink Slushie, the blood in the truck box crystalline and frozen. There were pink drops and red

Tracey Lindberg

blotches leading over the open end of the box and up the driveway. She followed them to the garage door. Nancy Drew would know what to do, but all she could think to do was to climb up the snow piled on the side of the garage between her house and the Olsons' and peek in the window.

The party was now a post-hunt party. Terry, her uncle Larry, her dad, Colin Ratt, Leonard Auger and Billy Morin sat on milk crates around an inky black moose. She saw that the beer had made it into the garage and that the men were flushed and talking with lots of gestures and movement. Terry laughed and tipped her head back at something her dad whispered to her. She went to grab a beer and bent over right in front of her dad.

"Bimbo." She breathed onto the small glass pane, fogging it up instantly. The frost covered Terry's miniskirted legs.

There was plastic on her dad's workshop tables, which had been pushed together, and there was a big roll of brown butcher's paper on the cement floor.

The men, as if receiving a signal, moved towards the moose. The garage tilted and blurred towards her as she saw the flashing of a knife in her uncle's hand. He skinned the moose cleanly and quickly, leaving the nose. The nose is a delicacy, she knew, and they would have it at feast. Steam rose off the still warm moose as cold air hits its nakedness. Terry grabbed a knife, like a prisoner on a prison break, and grabbed the moose's ear. The blood clouds Bernice's eyes and she retched, missing herself and hitting the lilac shrub. She sat down and watched the brown Cokey liquid freeze to the sparse bare branches of the tree like tiny ornaments on a Christmas tree.

Sometime later, she heard her mom calling her name and after that she felt her arms around her.

"Come inside, my girl, you've been gone so long." She peeked in the window. "They enjoy this more than they should." Her voice sounded funny and as she clung to her mother, she thought she saw tears sparkling in her tired liquid brown eyes.

Bernice was put in a hot bath, her mom squeezed oranges into it.

Bernice kept adding hot water until the heater was empty. She pulled on her mom's Sturgeon Lake T-shirt and crawled into her own bed. Her mom had put an extra blanket on the bed and came in every once in a while to see if Bernice was asleep yet. She was achy and thought she might be sick, but she was too tired to talk.

Later, the sounds of heavy boots walking in the front door and pounding across the floor, to the freezer, she imagined, woke her up.

And later still, the clank of beer bottles being placed on the floor and the thump of boots removed as the party moves from the garage to the next house. She looked at the little clock her mom gave her for Christmas. It was four-thirty.

There was the sound of hushed talking and then louder arguing and she faintly heard her mom speaking harshly to her husband and then her brother. There was yelling and then some scuffling. Bernice was not sure how long this went on for, as she dozed, but she was awakened by the sound of the beer bottles clinking and a door slamming. Later, she woke and heard nothing, assumed everyone had passed out, and felt herself grow less nervous.

Ahhhhhhh. She misses her mom. The ache in her stomach grows and reaches her chest. Soon it will spill into her throat and well up in her eyes if she is not careful. That love, that love that runs through her veins rushing like a stream threatening to spill onto the flood plain was rich and thick. The memory stills her and her breathing, quite unnoticed, stops.

She can smell the dark in the room, hear the sounds of emptiness, and Bernice feels Freda's small body move onto the mattress. How long has she been . . . travelling ? She keeps her eyes closed but thinks she feels her cousin's eyes on her. That lasts a long time.

She feels Freda's agitation next to her as her cousin flips over, the old floor in Bernice's apartment barely sighing as if the movement punctuates a sentence filled with tired verbs and exhausted pronouns.

She wonders if Freda can even see her anymore, or if there is an empty space in the bed where she used to settle.

I'm not here, she thinks. *I've changed.*

4

WHERE SHE IS

kasakes: a glutton, one who eats a lot

pawatamowin
She dreamsmells almonds and pesto.

T HE SMELL IN THE LITTLE BAKERY is yeasty and rich and chases the aroma from her head. Lola must have made dinner buns in the night, Bernice thinks to herself. That was her job before . . . before she took to her bed. *With a sick headache,* she thinks, opening her eyes. And, while she doesn't miss getting up at four to bake, she realizes she has begun to miss the steady stream of chatter around her that customers brought into Lola's with them. She would rarely wait on anyone but was always pleased when someone was kind to her. Her legs ache a bit, like she has been sleeping outside or walking all night. In that continuum that now exists between her body (which she has come to think of as a shell) and her spirit (within which emotions, thoughts and memories layer over each other, tendrils of fog on a road), she recognizes that her body is emotively moving. Anyone watching her would think she was in the throes of a deep sleep and suffering from restless leg syndrome. In the tendrils, Bernice realizes there is remorse in her body and she is trying to kick it out. Her shell rejects remorse. Shame. Feeling bad over feeling good.

When she first arrived at Gibsons she behaved . . . well, she did not behave. Some mornings she awoke lying alone in her room. Some mornings she sat up with a start, realizing she was in some strange place with some strange person next to her. One morning she awoke next to a stinky man. There was something entirely unpleasant about the person in bed next to her. He had a military haircut – and god – he couldn't have been an active serviceman for some twenty years. It was a brush cut, salt-and-pepper hair splayed straight up and out for the world to see. He was no Jesse.

He was not even Nick Adonodis. He rolled over, farted, and she stiffened, bracing herself for the unpleasant feel of his touch or growl of his talk. The stench was unaccompanied and therefore welcomed.

She knows she shouldn't have gone to the motel with him. There are a lot of shouldn't haves. Drunk gin. Flirted. Talked to strangers. Drunk gin. Flirted with strangers who bought her gin. It really was a limited and vicious circle. The first drink was the hardest. Well, getting to the first drink was the hardest. She didn't allow herself the luxury of just one drink (or just one anything, for that matter). Getting over the guilt of being a dry drunk/drinker (because, let's face it, she was never going to admit it) cost the most. Beyond that, though, when the world turned rosy and her armour gelatinous it got easier and easier.

She drank. She drank and the lines between her and other people blurred. She could hug, express love, laugh at things that her sober self would not allow her, and dropped thinking for feeling. She drank to feel something like she feels now, wrapped in the mink blanket Freda has brought, peaceful in her wakesleep, and able to feel her past without experiencing it – able to see it without reliving it.

That helps, because some of it was really quite – humiliating? No. She refuses it, feeling her hands tighten on their own. Humbling. It felt to her like she had slept in that cheap hotel with that married man about a hundred times. Not really, but the feeling of that particular model of man would not leave her easily. Art? Al? She remembers his name had only one syllable – about all she could manage by midnight. Come to think of it, maybe that was why she went home with him, instead of his two-syllabled friend. His last name was one of the Christmas reindeers. Well, it really doesn't matter anyhow, she supposed.

It was clear to her from the start that this was no ordinary guy. A skinny white dishevelled man hanging out at an Indian bar (how come they all have imperial names, she wonders: King George, The Empire Hotel, The Lord Tupper, The Royal?) was not such an odd thing. That he was somewhat attractive and well dressed was something of an oddity. But, when she looked into those eyes, those blue eyes (what colour were Knud Rasmussen's eyes?), she saw that something was amiss. What it was became clear soon enough, but at the time it just looked like near-crazy. Quasi-nuts. Pseudo-maniacal.

And while he was generically white-guy attractive, she had never been that attracted to generic. Or white guy. Or attractive guys. He honed in on her the moment he saw her. Then: she thought it was her spirit. Now: she knows it was blood in the bar water that drew him like a shark. Before she sank, back when she was willing to sleep with Art/Als, during the time of the shark, she didn't know that you couldn't really bury your pain and fear. And. While they were not the largest part of her, they rose to the surface like soured cream in coffee.

In the discord that floats through bad barrooms thicker than cigarette smoke and which runs faster than the beer on tap, her radar for mean was off.

That morning. The morning of Art/Al? she was a particular mess. Her shift at Lola's was starting in twenty minutes. Time enough to wash him off and out of her and get to the bakery. If she ran. Which she didn't. Opting to go unnoticed, she did the sneak. Pulled him close and flipped over – no small task for her two-hundred-plus-pound frame. He growled in his sleep (she seemed to recall that he growled in his wakened state as well). Taking care not to tip over the gin bottle, she had pulled on her 3X panties, 2X denim skirt and size 5 shoes. Picked up her purse, the gin bottle and his wallet. And left Art/Al to his humming, farting and snoring.

She stirs and feels sweat on her skin, the sheets wet with too much of some sense she doesn't understand. Sinks lower. Further. Shark cage. Recalls the thoughts in her head as she escaped the dirty motel and the old man.

One time when Skinny Freda was eighteen and she and Bernice had started spreading the space that existed between them in terms of size, Freda took her cousin to a house party (rather, a motel party) in High Prairie. Bernice had been struck silent as her cousin left the room every so often with a much older man and came back looking more and more dishevelled each time. When Freda looked for her in the morning (she had hidden herself by lying on the floor between the bed and the wall) the old white man, smelling of used clothing store and vomit, had said to her, "You will never find a squaw who doesn't wanna be found." She looked up to see Skinny Freda kick him in the groin, wink at her in her hiding spot and tell her, "Let's lose this loser, Bernice."

Remembering that, the fear of her own loser finding her, had lit a fire under Bernice as she made her way to work that day.

She actually did run then, throwing Art/Al's wallet out after she took his twenty-two dollars (if he hadn't slapped her, she would never have considered taking it). Breathless and sweating, she had opened the bakery door and heard Lola in the back, smoking and singing a song that Bernice recognized as a song that Cher sings. Lola was pretty fond of Cher. And Sonny, for Pete's sake and what that meant. Liking Sonny told Bernice something about Lola that Bernice couldn't quite figure out. It wasn't good, though.

"I knocked twice, figured you had a late night," Lola said to her, not commenting on the alternative. "You look . . ." – she had paused for effect because effect was all and cause was irrelevant to Lola – "like you got the worst of it."

Bernice marched by her, too-short denim skirt accentuating the broken strap on her Walmart shoes. When she saw herself in the stainless steel oven reflection she realized she had blood on her lip. And, strangely enough, in her eye.

She didn't remember getting hit in the eye.

"Some men don't know when a woman . . ." Lola began, but Bernice was already on her way upstairs to shower and change. She had wondered for not the first time whether living so close to work was such a great idea.

She had felt resentful then, the arrangement making her lie, ". . . tripped on the way home. Slept at a friend's. Be right back."

Lola knew the truth. Not because Lola presumed bad deeds. But because Lola knew Bernice had no friends. She didn't even have a telephone, and no phone calls came to the bakery for her. At that point, Bernice had lived in Gibsons for almost a month and not once had there been an inkling that she had any life outside of the bread she baked, cheesecake she prepared or pastries she delivered.

In fact, Lola knew nothing about Bernice. One time she caught Lola looking in the trash bag that she delivered to the back of the store. She could still see it – Lola's spidery polyester legs poking out of the red dumpster in the back alley. She imagined the surprised look on the old woman's face at the balled-up wad of old newspaper clippings and pictures of Jesse from *The Beachcombers*. She kept only two.

When she stepped into the shower – it was more of a hose running up the front of the tub, where there were tiles as high as her shoulders – she had let the cold water splash her. There was no hot water in the apartment but she grew used to it. She used glycerine soap to cleanse. Started with her arms and breasts. Cleaned her parts and then the rest of herself. She had no idea what she looked like. Had no knowledge of her body. The rivulets of ice water fell on foreign terrain, crisscrossed everywhere by stretch marks. She went to wash her long hair but remembered at the last minute she had cut it. The braid sat in a basket in the corner of the bathroom – right where she left it when she got the news from home that her mom had left and she sheared herself.

It only took a second to wash her hair after that. Most of the time she didn't bother.

Lola had banged on her ceiling, the noise reverberating through the floor of Bernice's apartment. Bernice knew it was a sneaker on a broom handle. She also knew it was approaching six o'clock. She lingered, the feel of Art/Al? dripping off.

She hoped that she was careful and that she didn't tell him where she worked.

Lola was tap tap tapping her cigarette as she rolled herself a fresh one. Bernice had come to value soundlessness. Some days, entire days, she would not speak to anyone. Not even silencetalking. She didn't answer the voice that was moving around in her head. Regardless of where and who she was. It never occurred to her then that she might have been sick. That her silence was unhealthy. That her speech may have had value. That the pain of death needed to be released. Most of the time, when she did talk, it was in her bad Cree.

"Mah," she chided, when she had done something clumsy. The word floated like a willow seed to the ground. Sometimes she thought her words moved out of her way, light enough to be airborne, when she swept the flour, sugar and baking powder from the floor at night. Other times, like the day she felt her mom was gone, they sat heavily and would not move, no matter how much she swept. Her arms were leaden too, sawing at her hair for what seemed like hours, before the give of the final strands left her holding her braid and staring at it without recognition.

"Go to bed, my girl," Lola said to her that night in Bernice's own language, and they had both looked at each other hard because Lola does not speak Cree. For that one gift, Bernice let Lola order her down the stairs today.

"Did you hear?" Lola let her words bounce, like they had places to go, even though she knew Bernice had pulled the cord of the radio from the wall.

"Some computer whiz kid shut down the radar at the Vancouver airport. Planes almost crashing everywhere."

To her, Lola had seemed dismayed that no one had crashed yet. Sometimes Bernice thought mean thoughts and didn't take them back. Other times she thought good thoughts and let them powder the room – just in case there was a running count on them. Also, it gave the ugly thoughts a soft place to land.

It came to her that maybe she was losing touch. Not with reality – a place where she was often a visitor – but she was actually losing her sense of human feeling. She looked at her hands, soft from the butter and lard, and noticed that even though she had placed them on the oven door, they felt no heat.

". . . and I told the girls this would happen with all of that newfangled computer chips," Lola pronounced proudly.

"Hmmmm," Bernice said.

Other times she would say "interesting" or "wow" but on that day she couldn't find any words to take the places of the ones she puts out there so she only hummed. On that day, the voices and the shift were hovering around her like summer fog on grass after a rain. She remembers thinking of Art/Al? puffing over her and of her fear that he would have a stroke on top of her. She wonders what she would have done then.

"You have a nice time last night?" Lola asked her, unkindly, and would have been hurt if you suggested she was being unkind.

Bernice tried to hum again, surprised by the question.

"Yes." She was living a secret life inside her head, she thought. She remembered when she and Skinny Freda used to wonder about the secret life of cows. Some days they would take Freda's beat-up truck out onto the open road and honk to see if cows would respond. They never did until that last cold Sunday before she left. She was on a day pass from the San and Freda and she went for a drive in the country.

Tracey Lindberg

Reaching a pasture, they were delighted to find that one cow looked up at them when the horn tweaked. She and Freda finished their Cokes and went home. They have not spoken since. She feels like the cow sometimes – like it was chance or some strange unexpected expected response that sometimes fuelled her. As a reactor and not an actor, when Lola spoke to her she sometimes found herself responding, even though she had dwindling capacity for interaction. Lola, still impatiently wondering about Bernice's evening, had continued to ask questions – completely unaware that her employee was travelling right in front of her.

"Makin' some new friends?" Lola tweaked, twisting her cigarette-stained hand in a mime of some act Bernice didn't want to recognize.

But did.

"A couple."

"Men friends?"

"A few."

"Anyone you'll bring home to meet your old pal Lola?"

Home. Like they lived in this extended oven. She wanted to lie but found that space emptied.

"Not likely." Over time, she had found that her capacity to lie had diminished. If she could get away without speaking, she would never have to lie.

"Oh, the type you don't bring home to . . ."

Bernice's head had filled the room with the sounds of flames flickering. She could hear nothing else. Lola's lips moved and expectation flooded her face, but Bernice was already mixing and pouring, stirring and folding.

One day a letter came from her *kohkom* to the bakery. *Kohkom* was the only person Bernice ever told where she had gone. She had also told her in Cree, as if it couldn't come into the white world if it was spoken in their language. The letter was in Freda's handwriting and Bernice knew *Kohkom* had Skinny Freda write down everything that she said. Reading it was just like listening to her. Her mother was gone (and Bernice tries hard not to think *dead and gone*). Or gone dead. The letter didn't say. It didn't matter, she had felt as much. Still, she worried about her *kohkom* having to say it and Freda having to write it. No one knew where Maggie was, Freda had translated.

Bernice knew the truth, though. She had killed her mother. Carrying Bernice's secrets had been too much for her mother. She shouldn't have told her the truth. Shouldn't have gone to Maggie in her sleep. Shouldn't have given her the shame in a dreambundle. Should have let her think she just ran away. But it was too late and there was no one left to carry that bundle except her. A couple of times she was going to tell Freda about it, but changed her mind just as the ugly words tore at the back of her lips to get out. When she left for the San she could have told Freda so she could take care. Instead, she breathed in deeply and held the breath until she squirmed too much and saw stars. Everyone knows too much oxygen can smother unwanted words. And now she is glad she did breathe because those words would have killed Skinny Freda just like they killed her mom.

She was fidgety then, she thinks, like her insides were squirming to fit her outsides. Or her outsides were trying to find the person that formerly occupied them. Lola stared at her.

Spoke words she could not hear. Bernice had soothed herself by running her fingers through her hair and was surprised, once again, at its shortness. At that time, it had grown out three or four inches since she cut it. It is now at her shoulders again, but when Lola saw what she had done she marched her right over to Shear Talent to get the ends evened out. Bernice can't remember who paid. Maybe it was one of those kindnesses that Lola heaps on her that can't actually be felt or measured – so much so that you don't actually notice it. Like the free meals. Like not smacking her gum or speaking too loudly around her. Like when she coaxed Bernice into her '74 Malibu and pretended she was not looking for Pat John's house. How shocked he would have been to see an emaciated sixty-two-year-old in teal tights and red lipstick and an ample Cree woman in baker's whites parked by the road in front of his house.

With a jolt, she noticed Lola was gesticulating and miming something she and the girls did in Reno last year. Bernice had heard the story already and stared at Lola, only to hear the sound of a crackling fire as wind whipped flames.

"Okay, get me a pack of Salems, too," Lola had said, reaching for her purse.

"What?"

"You said 'cigarettes,' kid, just like ya' were a smoker yourself."

"I thought you were cutting down."

"Not today. Make them lights, okay?" She tried to hand Bernice a ten.

"I've got money." She had grabbed Art/Al?'s twenty-two dollars and walked next door to Ralph's convenience store.

The sounds of Lola and Freda's laughter drift up the stairs. She is sensitive to sound now and wonders when that started. She has wolf ears, she thinks, smiling a bit behind her face. Maybe it's being housed in the same small room for so long, but she feels like all of her sensepowers are sharper. She can tell when Freda is on her time. She knows, with precision, when the sun will rise and set. She can tell when Freda is sneaking up the stairs, hoping to catch her . . . what? Awake? Alive? In her skin?

She knows, though, Bernice thinks, *that I am not my self as much. Anymore.*

Accepting this as her truth, she closes her eyes and does not sleep. But. Moves.

❧

Freda was always the spitting image of Maggie. It used to bother Bernice that this tiny little woman had come from another mother and still was more closely related to Maggie than she could ever be. Freda was born looking like a wizened old woman and even, sometimes, resembled one now, but when she was young, her cousin and Maggie used to sit together in the lodge, the space between her mother and herself occupied by the mini-Maggie doppelgänger. While it bothered her, Bernice had accepted it as natural, that she could in no way take the space of niecedaughter next to the tiny mom whom she had eclipsed in size at age ten.

Tracey Lindberg

Perhaps what was most paining was that Maggie was able to express warmth to Freda in ways that she could not to her own daughter. Bernice watched as her mom smoothed out Freda's hair, patted her brow on occasion and took her hand in public. In this, Bernice knew her mom was demonstrating motherlove for her motherless cousin. It was warm and generous. But, she still felt like her mother's ability to love more than one child at once was meagre. In truth, Freda was a lovable kid. Talkative, interested and light, words rushed out of her like river water on stones. Bernice, who found herself difficult to love, had always believed that her mom could not love her. Could not love BigHer. Could not find enough love within her to spread around.

When she said as much to her Auntie Val, the bigwoman-sisterlittlemother had patted her hand. "No. Birdie. No. She doesn't love Freda more. She loves you too much to treat you like that."

Bernice had never known what that meant until she found a bird, still on the ground, after hitting their picture window. She fed it and watered it, watched it for hours and prayed for it to heal. She would not touch it, though. She wanted it to find its kin and fit in again without her tainting it.

And, in truth, Bernice harbours none of the fearanger and rage that seemed to sit on Maggie's and Freda's skin like a bruise. Bernice's injury was more akin to the internal injuries sustained from a crash. They pained, were always there and could manifest at any time. For the most part, they stayed beneath the surface. Unobserved.

Freda's rage was more accessible and evident than Maggie's,

certainly. She had a hair-trigger temper (and later, a rye-trigger temper) that flamed and snuffed easily. While Maggie's would burn less often, the intensity of it was so familiar to Bernice that she grew fearful when she didn't feel it.

There was a time when Bernice could feel that rage in her mom every day. When Freda stayed with them there was the hum of a potential anger storm. Even she could not get a read on Maggie's rage. Bernice could, though. The house would grow fat with acrimony; the air pungent with rancour. Her eyes would sting with the vinegariness of malignity. Bernice didn't know quite where it came from, but there were two distinct eventualities that arose from it. Auntie Val would come over while Maggie took to her bed. She lavished Bernice and Freda with praise, food and hugs. A second effect: Freda moved from Maggie's house to Val's and became her daughter. No one ever mentioned it. No one ever talked about a lot of things. What happened to Freda's mom. Why Freda lived with everyone at one time or another. Why Maggie stopped talking to anyone. When the electricity would come back on. Why no one stayed with the uncles. The silence about what was happening around them seeped into the kitchen, first. Permeating the curtains. Eating into the linoleum. Eventually settling in the fridge. It was like some sort of bad medicine – it made Freda skinny, Bernice fat, and Maggie disappear.

In her mind, which feels oddly sharp and awake in the haze and among the bedclothes, Bernice recalls Freda disappearing for weeks on end. Then, she would show up, all scrubbed up and made up, at Maggie's with tight clothes on and hickeys on her neck. Once in a while on these visits to her old home,

Tracey Lindberg

Maggie would look through Bernice, catch sight of something familiar in Freda and pause. Bernice couldn't understand it but there was some sort of challenge going on, like Freda was daring Maggie to see her again. Maggie just stared, though. Never said a word. Never raised a telling eyebrow.

Over time, things between Freda and Maggie became like things between Maggie and everyone. A quiet acceptance that this was the way she would be now. The only proof that they had ever been mother and daughter was the angst Bernice carried with her that her mom could give her up, too, at any time.

Bernice's skin feels electric; the pale cool sheets seem to sizzle around her. This. This is unknown to her. She is not sure, but believes that if she sat up she would be spring-like. This. This is anger.

acimowin

The Storyteller chuckles and says
Just before she wakes, the owl,
she is flying over
a forest and sees that all of the trees
have died. All of the trees
except one.
She flies over it and poops.

5

MANY TRIPS, MANY SUFFERINGS

misiwanacihow: someone who fell victim to suffering

pawatamowin
*In the old dream, the one she kept having when she lived at home
– when there was a home – she was too fat to get into the sweatlodge. But she does get in and sits near the door on the women's
side – a place of honour – but only because she knew that if she
ventured past the women in the lodge she would fall into the fire.
She was the last person in and it was a full house – her legs were
pressed too tightly together.*

Flesh folded on flesh.

*A man, an invisible and too near her man, was passing the
pipe to her. She had to reach over the empty space in front of the
door. Her arms felt heavy and dough-like and she had to heave her
weighted self towards him to grasp, too roughly, the offered pipe.*

She is seated by her Auntie Val and Skinny Freda. There was a
moniaskwew* *seated right beside them, but the woman didn't look like
anyone she knows. Everyone was real quiet, listening to a Storyteller.*

* White woman.

THINKFEELING IT NOW, Bernice would have to say that the change had started in Edmonton. She went there after she left the San. She didn't sink; she skipped on the water. First, she started to dream in black-and-white. Not just any black-and-white, but Charlie Chaplin, old film new machine black-and-white. Stilted motions and pantomimed facial expressions, she could never quite understand what was being said as there was no sound in these dreams. No piano player to indicate the action is intensifying or that the emotion has deepened. Each morning since the movies started, well, every afternoon if truth be told, she had awakened with a too-familiar ache in her chest; the pain below her breastbone felt nothing like a bird. She couldn't discern if it was her conscience or her feelings that hurt, so she ignored it.

In the time before she truly sank, the dreams would linger with her throughout the day, almost forgotten, as she rushed to get out of her pyjamas and into whatever clothes were sitting nearest to the bed. Although they started when she was in Edmonton when she left the San, those dreams fill her now, floating in and out of the room whether she is awake or not. Now, she suspects that not inviting the dreams in made her a bit wonky in Alberta. (*Wonky and wonkier,* she often thought to herself, stifling a laugh.) But it was in Edmonton that her dream life and her waking life had begun to fold over each other, seamlessly, like dough in a pan. In order to maintain what she understood as normal, she found that she had to be very quiet. She stifled a lot, then. It is strange, while immobile now, she feels more awake, aware and engaged than she ever has. She stifles nothing. But then. Then: loud laughs, too-big smiles and inappropriate questions at people on the street. She swallowed frank stares at, crazy thoughts about, and unsuitable gestures towards any person who happened to pass by her. The "trouble," as near as she could figure it, began almost as soon as she left the San. One day, she decided she was going to visit her Auntie Val. She had planned to stay with her, initially, but found the space between her dream and waking life too precarious and did not want to take that to her auntie's place. Her auntie had given her a key for her apartment the last time she visited Bernice at the San and she remembered it that morning. On that day, when she was changed, she walked down Jasper Avenue, waited at the bus stop and was sitting there when the line between dreaming and waking life seemed to blur – she became someone else. At first, she thought that she had made herself scarce, but on the second day of no eye contact and no acknowledgment, she knew the truth: she had made the change.

Her *kohkom** used to be able to do the change. When she got to the city and told people who her *kohkom* was, someone gave her a book about that. It was called *Shapeshifters* and it was filled with a whole bunch of phony-baloney stuff. There was, however, a picture of Rose Calliou, her *kohkom*, on page seventy-seven. *Kohkom* was squinting like she couldn't quite make out who was taking her picture. She had her hair in an ever-present braid, and if the sepia page had been in colour, she knows that the skirt, shirt and shawl would have matched only in their brightness and not their colour scheme. Rich purples, oranges and pinks filled *Kohkom's* wardrobe. Seeing

* *Kohkom* means "your/her/his grandmother." (*Nohkom* means "my grandmother.")

her flat and two-dimensional on the page had upset her and she felt like crying but didn't need to – by then, and not since she sank, she had cried so often that when she wasn't crying the space occupied by where the tears used to be felt like a phantom limb. So disconnected is she from her body, or perhaps so intertwined are emotion and body, that she is not sure she would know if she was crying. Pain currently registers in her skin and sorrow in her breasts. Whether that translates to tears or not is still something of which she is not aware. She knows, as well as she knows the indentation of that knife beneath her, that it could mean she is detached. She also thinks that she is registering and responding to the change in a way that lets her shroud and feel things as she needs to. It reminds her of cocooning – and the thought at once soothes her.

In Edmonton, still numb from the incessant thrum and howl of the San, she used to try and try to turn herself into a bug. She thought about wandering through the treacherous orange shag rug that Auntie Val had in her living room. She imagined she would be able to climb up the door jamb and out the window. Then she would imagine doing the change and becoming a butterfly and flying high high high until her breath was hard to find. She never imagined coming back. Auntie Val's apartment, unkindly regarded as "Pecker Palace" by the people who knew such things, was on a busy street between a convenience store that always smelled of spoiled hamburger (although they did not sell meat) and a halfway house for men. It served as a post house. Post-marriage, post–skid apartment, post–last bad job. What kept them from thinking of their home, their lives, their jobs as pre-anything was also something understood by those in the know. Now she thinks often about how much she hated going there, thinking of it as home. Then, she could not afford the luxury of disdain.

When she felt the change coming on that time, she found herself oddly teary all week. There was a sense of alteration, of movement, but she couldn't tell if it was that she had lost something or found something. Keeping her head up, inter-acting with the world in small ways made it clearer: some-thing had shifted. It wasn't as if she needed it quantified, but a general animal, vegetable or mineral categorization might have helped. Something about the San had altered her; it was like being amongst so many crazies had allowed her one crazy thought of her own: I can shift. With so many skewed, altered and created realities around her, Bernice no longer felt her foot tethered. To Here. Now. By the time she left for Edmon-ton she had a comfort in her that she had never known. It was Edmonton where she learned how to skip on the water. Pres-ently, it is not hard to imagine how she got Here. It is infinitely more difficult to understand what Here is. It is not the soiled Sealy, the smell of sweatsadness or Freda and Lola's endless "pop ins" to see if she has moved. Eaten. Changed. She wants to tell them that the change is precisely the thing. She knew she could change by the time she left the San, but the story of the change started in Edmonton, is too much to tell, and can't possibly be translated to there. That bed, that room, that bakery. Here started on Edmonton public transit.

On that day, the day when she shifted entirely, she got on the Edmonton City Centre bus, its exhaust pouring out like the steam from a dragon's mouth. She was the last one to get on. Walking unevenly to the back of the bus, and trying to balance her bigself as the city bus pulled away from the curb, her skin, she remembers, felt alive and ancient. She sat across from two old women who were speaking a language she didn't recognize. It sounded throaty and nasally like Blackfoot but the language also felt liquid and had the rich cadence of Dene, so she couldn't place it. Every so often the old women would pepper their conversation with terminology for which there must not be translations. "Microwave," one woman said between a rush of other words. The other old woman nodded and smiled, smiled and nodded. There was comfort in their familiarity with each other. She felt the longing for the women in her family so acutely that it gnawed at her like a presence.

Back home, sometimes the grandmothers would gather for tea and whatever they were working on together. They would talk about their children and grandchildren in Cree. Every so often words would come out that had no Cree translation. "Satellite dish!" one of her grandmothers would pronounce. *Kohkom* would smile and nod, nod and smile. Those children and grandchildren who had moved to the city got special mention and a firmness in the lips when they were discussed. Back then, she believed that this was an indication that moving away from home – be it the rez or the town next to it – was a failure of sorts. Once she had made the move to the big city and become a big shot (the only two times when "big" had a pejorative meaning) she re-wrote the firm lips and the deliberate mention of relocation. She equated the city, once she lived there, with jobs and resources that don't exist in Little Loon.

Tracey Lindberg

That day on the bus, when it lurched to a stop and picked up a family, she watched as a young mom had difficulty getting her stroller up the steps. One of The Kids was a short and pudgy boy about three years old. His face was smeared with grape something and he seemed to be still enjoying it. Another of the children was a little older, but not by much, she thought, with two long black braids hanging to his waist. There were four kids in all. Every one of them had a runny nose.

Cluck cluck cluck said an old woman with her tongue against the roof of her mouth but without opening it. Nod and frown, frown and nod said the other. Bernice realized without surprise that she was becoming someone else, someone who could speak without talking. The change took her voice and gave her a new talk (that this new talk could include old white woman Ukrainian did not give her pause).

The woman with The Kids had sat next to her and said, Oh it's cold on here! Her lips didn't move and Bernice had wondered how she had learned to talk this way.

Yeah, the newer ones have heaters all the way to the back though, Bernice answered her.

Just as well, they need to keep bundled anyhow, the mother said, pointing in her kids' direction with her lips.

Must be Cree, Bernice thought.

You from the city? the woman asked her.

No, up north, Bernice answered.

I thought so, did I see you at Little Loon?

Probably, my mom lives there, well, in Big Valley.

Bernice looked her in the eye. You from here?

Woman with four kids laughed a big laugh, so hard her

belly shook a little. No my old man and I moved here from Poundmaker's in the spring, he hopes to find work. She shifted her ample bottom on the seat to half-face Bernice. I told him there wasn't no use – nobody in Edmonton's gonna hire one of us. Bernice smiled and nodded.

You got a job? She pointed at Bernice.

No, I am going to visit my aunt.

The two old white women looked at Bernice distrustfully, she thought. Maybe they thought she had deceived them by not being Indian with them right away. She looked at her reflection in the half-window of the bus that was closed. Long brown hair, high cheekbones and medium tone. She was medium. At least, that's what she had been told at the cop shop. Why do they want your colour listed, anyhow? she had thought. Old ladies whispered with lips moving to themselves, now afraid to let even a little of their secret language be shared with the other women on the bus.

The cold air whistling through the bus was quite unbearable. She wished she had worn a hat and scarf. Her threadbare gloves were no match for the biting cold. She pulled the cord, the effort of raising her arm through her heavy coat and sweater draining the last of her energy. She pulled her purse to her side, picked up her Thermos and got off the bus. She gathered the last remnant of her strength and readied herself for the three-block walk to the Pecker Palace.

There were no trees to shield her from the wind. She cut through a back alley, it was shorter that way, and was surprised to see another woman taking the alley shortcut. It was late now and it was dark. One thought crossed her mind: What is the big awful, so terrible that walking through a putrid alley alone, at night, seems safe? It was thirty below and her breath formed a foggy halo above her head as she walked. She was going full speed when she tripped over them. Deer legs. Finding them in the city surprised her. Finding them unused and discarded surprised her even more. At home the legs would be used for sausage. In the big city, they were litter. Although it was cold, she thought she could smell the hide smell.

She had tanned hides with *Kohkom* as long as she could remember. *Kohkom* would speak to her only in Cree, even though her mom had told the old lady not to. It seemed to Bernice that she could understand everything *Kohkom* said, although today she could not remember a word of Cree. They would scrape scrape scrape the remaining tissue, meat and fat from the hide, *Kohkom* with a deer bone, Bernice with a fashioned bed leg. The smell of the fat on her hands was strong and almost putrid. Nowadays, they had to keep the hides in a freezer and then thaw them out. Kind of like killing them twice, *Kohkom* told her. The smell was from freezing, thawing and freezing, not like the old days, *Kohkom* said in Cree. Bernice wondered silently if in the old days *Kohkom* used a wringer washer to soak the hides in like she did now. Wisely, she kept her mouth shut.

When she walked by that family's house, the family who had the legs, she wondered what they did with the rest of the deer. She wondered if they ate any of it, or if they tanned the hide. Most likely, they sent the hide to a taxidermist and didn't eat the meat. Bernice and her aunt could have used the meat.

Auntie Val made a lot of rice, noodle or potato casseroles.

She ate bannock every day, and not always with jam. "This is nothing," Auntie told her, unapologetically, the last time they visited. "We used to take bannock and lard to school and that's all we had. Your uncle Larry," she would always lower her voice at this point, "used to skip his meal and give it to the younger ones."

As she walked up the path and then steps of Val's apartment she glanced around to make sure that no one saw her enter with her own key. Twenty of the Pecker Palace apartments were owned by the Native Co-op, and if they thought that Bernice lived there, Auntie Val's rent would go up by one. The Co-op conducted periodic inspections, the stated purpose being making sure that the wiring and heating were okay, but every so often when she visited, Bernice would have to pack fast and leave. It was annoying, but Val paid only ninety dollars a month in rent for a pretty good place.

She walked in and the smell of fresh bread and buns wrapped around her and hugged her. Auntie Val always baked on nights as cold as that one.

When she opened the door, she spoke to her auntie in her new, non-voice. Auntie, I'm home, she whispered, brushing deer fur off her pants.

"Is someone there?" Auntie Val asked.

Auntie Val, Bernice had understood, could no longer see or hear her.

She remembers going to the living room and sitting there for the night, the sounds of sirens, which usually bothered her, became a sweet low cadence. Even now, wide awake and eyes closed, she can remember thinking that nothing in her had altered, that something outside of her had. If she were able to speak of it now, she would say that the world shifted, not she. That colours felt like tastes and sounds poured like liquid. It was something that started There and which became Here. At that time, in the city, she had no idea what she looked like or where she was when she changed. It didn't occur to her that the day held any special meaning.

Now, with the luxury of being here, she understands that the change may have happened completely that night, but pieces of it started earlier. Those changes started in her body. When she was sixteen Bernice first began to feel the dissonance between her active life and her inner life. She had no body knowledge, and no one but her cousin Freda talked to her once she left home, so she had no barometer for normal. She remembers feeling this disconnected before, when she was little and in the same apartment. Her auntie had taken her to live with her in Grandetowne. Every day Bernice would walk from the south hill of Big Valley to the north flats, spending her days in a religious all-white girls' school and her nights in a (then) all-white neighbourhood. Just a few hours' drive from the relative quiet of her community, she felt estranged from familiar faces and sounds. Felt that she would die if she went to Loon but that she was not living there either.

When Freda moved out, first from Maggie's place and then from Val's, a spark of something left the house at Little Loon. Once her mom had left, it felt like there was no air left in the house. So, she went to live with her auntie, for the first time. Auntie Val was still partying then and Bernice remembers doing most things alone in Grandetowne. Shopping for groceries. Getting smokes for Val. Making her lunches. Walking to school.

What is her normal, that which sits in the bed with her, was once foreign to Bernice. Her heels dig into the frayed sheets, almost imperceptibly, as she sees herself trying to make the transition from There to Here. Often, she recalls, she could hear the grandmothers whispering to her as she walked along the path to that school. For a long time she thought she was crazy, hearing voices and all, but she came to know that this was regular and normal for her. She remembers that she had stopped to buy a Coke from Lou's! corner store. Lou, or some Lou-looking man, as always, eyed her warily. No big deal, she was used to it. Still, she is certain she had to stifle the urge to stick her tongue out at him.

Cutting through the courthouse parking lot and looking towards the steps (where busy-looking men in business-looking suits walk quickly in and out of the doors) Bernice had always felt an increasing sense of dread every time she took a step closer to school. The courthouse was perched on top of the hill. When she reached the top she looked down at Big Valley with all of its varied splendour. The heat rose with purpose from the blackened asphalt urged forcefully into the potholes along the road.

She could see the A&W sign to the north peeking up from behind the mall. At that time, her Auntie Val lived across the street from the restaurant. It was a drive-in then. When Bernice's mom left she had dropped her off to live with Val, and the three of them walked over and sat in the one booth located inside of the restaurant and ordered cheap hamburgers and

Tracey Lindberg

coffee. The memory is fat with meaning that she can't decipher, and as she captures the moment in her mind she hears a bird-like trill come from her throat and compete with the noise of the bakery for a place to land.

She knows that they did not talk.

Once they were done and got outside, Maggie had asked Bernice if she was full. She answered that she was because even if she was hungry then there was nothing that could be done about it and she didn't want her mom to feel bad. Auntie Val offered her a cough drop, they walked across the street to the rundown apartment block (no security door or lock to impede their progress) and walked up the rickety stairs to Valene's apartment in the Pecker Palace. It was, she remembers, a room with many doors. Instead of walls, the apartment had doors that led directly to the main hallway. She used to pretend that the doors led to exotic places: islands with palm trees, castles with hidden rooms, or caves with treasure buried within. This was hard to sustain when drunks pounded on the door mistakenly. Those times she had just wished the doors led to other rooms. Rooms with locks.

She remembers her mom hugging her and telling her to be good. To be a good helper to her auntie. To try to fit in. In her little room at Lola's, she knows she has never and will likely never fit in anywhere. She can feel that hug. The warmth. Res-ignation. There was no finality in that hug. Her mom took a last look around the apartment before leaving and said, "I'm going to make you some curtains." Bernice had wondered anxiously when they would get the window coverings, when her mom would come again, when she would come to get her for good. So she could go with her. To. Someplace. Some new place. Some home.

Once she moved in with her aunt, the apartment seemed no less forlorn, but she got used to it. Every school day she walked down the hill and then turned left at the Sears store at the base of the hill. There were never exhibits in the Sears store windows, but she often saw people milling about, even during the week, looking for a bargain. No one looked at her and she had begun to feel happily invisible.

When she walked the last four blocks to school, she began to count her steps. Almost always, she walked eight hundred and seventy-four steps, but some days she would take tiny steps to see how many it would take if she was smaller or older. At eight hundred and seventy she reached the sidewalk before the walkway leading to the school. She was at Christ's Academy for three years. Someday, her mom had told her, she would go to a school where there were boys. She never minded their absence but couldn't tell her mom that. She remembers dragging her feet up the stairs and hearing the grandmothers telling her to go straight to class. Some days she had wanted to ignore them, wanted to walk straight past the Academy. With her blue blazer and plaid skirt, though, she knew she was likely to be spotted. Instead, each day she went to her locker, opened it and put her *maskihky** bag inside. She took care to wrap the leather thong gently around the small rectangular leather bag and place it in the corner.

One day Sister Marie Thérèse had asked her what was in the bag, in front of the entire history class. She told the Sister

* Medicine.

Tracey Lindberg

that it was a sacred bag – that's what the grandmothers told her – and Sister Marie Thérèse sent her to Sister Mary Margaret's office. The stern principal demanded an explanation for the bag.

She remembers the grandmothers telling her to keep quiet.

Be still, Birdie, they told her as she wriggled in her chair. She wriggles in her bed at the memory. At the discomfort. At the detainment.

They used to cut our hair, they reminded each other.

Remember when they beat us for speaking our language, they whispered to each other in Cree. Sometimes, Bernice still hears them whispering to each other.

She sees herself as she was then, a chubby fine-boned Halfbreed girl, nervously swinging her legs and brushing her long hair out of her eyes. In her mind's eye, she sees her legs abruptly stop moving, her features become sharper and a subtle ruffling of her arms. The new plaid skirt cutting the air with its tightly pressed edges.

"Take that bag off!" Sister had ordered.

Run! the grandmothers told her. Don't let her touch the medicine! they reminded her.

She had run all the way to the apartment. It was only 10:30 in the morning and she wasn't allowed to have a key. She sat still in the scorching summer sun, her uniform becoming drenched and heavy with perspiration, until her aunt came home.

She was semi-delirious by that point.

Auntie Val had, with the dignity the Creator placed in big wimmins, marched to the "Jesus Christly school" muttering something about humility, charity and nunbitches. Bernice ate a box of fake Honeycombs, a row of crackers and a half-jar of generic Cheez Whiz before her auntie came back.

After that, the Sisters had been really nice to her.

One day, on that most particular of days, Bernice had walked into her classroom and looked at the clock. It was 8:53. Class started at 8:55 and she was almost never late. She was almost too early. When the bell rang, she remembers, the other twelve-year-old girls skipped gaily to the front of the class to hold hands and pray.

"Oh Heavenly Father," the classroom intoned.

Creator of all, the grandmothers prayed serenely.

The white girls continued, "We ask you for forgiveness for our sins . . ."

She could not hear them over the grandmothers who reminded her to say thank you for this beautiful day. She thinks now that this was a lovely way to start the day, if you left out all the Jesus and fear and just talked to your Creator about thankfulness. She learned to pray in her own way in that room. Something tweaks in her now, her heels imperceptibly undig from the foot of the bed, and Bernice knows that something in her shifted at Christ's Academy. She doesn't know what it was, but she does know that in time, all she could hear was the quiet murmur of *iskwewak*.*

When they were done their prayers, the school children settled in for a day of lessons taught by the Sisters. She listened carefully to their teachings because the old ones told her this would be important to her and her family someday.

At recess she took her lunch and wandered to the highest

* Cree women, Indian women.

Tracey Lindberg

point of the schoolyard where a few girls seated themselves, two by two. She got to the very top and sat down, making sure that she did not wrinkle her skirt or dirty her white socks. She had pride in that uniform. Most girls had two, but she had one. Before she moved Bernice to the city, her mother had been very quiet when she read the card that had the prices for uniform rentals. The Academy had recommended that each student rent three uniforms. She knew she would only have one. She heard her auntie on the phone at the laundromat beside their apartment one afternoon. She knew by the wrinkle in Val's forehead that she was talking to her uncles. They had not spoken for some time and Bernice knew it was hard for her to ask them for anything.

"For Chrissake, Larry, there is no one else," Valene had hissed. Her long black hair was piled on her head and she was wearing a big turquoise T-shirt, Bernice remembers. There is one just like it in her little closet. Lola told her, last time she wore it, that she was swimming in it.

"No. No. No. I don't know, Larry. No one knows. She said she would come to visit the next long weekend." Bernice had wondered at the time if Auntie was talking about her mom. Now, she knows.

Valene looked angry, annoyed, a little hungover and something else that Bernice does not know yet, in her little room over the bakery, and she will not be able to identify that piece of her auntie for years. "Just send the fucking money, Larry." Bernice imagines her eyebrows must have flown off her little-girl face. Gritted teeth and set jaw displaying a fierceness she wished she'd known when her daughterniece was young. When she thought she knew. When she could have done something. One thing. "You fuckers owe her that."

Two weeks later, three crumpled twenty-dollar bills came in a dirty white envelope addressed to Bernice at her auntie's. There was no note from her mom. She had wondered at the time if that money came from her uncle but quickly put it out of her mind. She had folded the envelope carefully and placed it in her underwear drawer where no one would find it. They had cared for that uniform like it was a precious stone, cleaning it frequently and looking at it in something like wonder. For this reason, and not because she only had one, Bernice had always been careful to sit like a lady when she wore the uniform.

When she would sit on the hill, she pretended she was in the woods up north. She had a favourite spot about a mile from their home; a place directly between the town and Loon Lake. She would walk through a field thick with wild grass, weeds and the sweetest-smelling flowers. She had to go through the Williers' yard to get there and was afraid of the rez dogs that hid from the sun under the trampoline. Sometimes they would follow her amiably, but one time they eyed her warily and curved their lips in a smilesnarl. After that she carried a walking stick with her in case she needed to shoo them away. In the fall, shots would ring out as the men from the community hunted for moose. The cacophonous noise was at once nerve-racking and soothing to her with its power and familiarity. From that hill, how she missed that hill now, she could see the Williers' and their relations' homes to the south, the Omeasoos' to the north and the Cardinals' to the east. Her family's home and a few others were scattered (back to back where that could happen) about the west end of the reserve but not on it. With only one of their family members entitled to a house on the tiny reserve (an uncle who lived in the city) the Meetoos family made no complaints about the house or the land they were effectively squatting on until the only legal Indian in their family decided he wanted his house back. Her vantage point from the hill up north told a story of belonging and intolerance that she could not quite understand yet. The hill dwarfed the one at the school, but when she was there she would try to generate that same feeling of belonging/alienation that was familiar enough to resonate with home.

She remembers girls screeching, running, thumping and laughing. She remembers opening her lunch kit and taking out the note from her mom that her Auntie Val placed there.

Remember you are my little brown dolly. Be strong and good.
Love mom

She had shredded the paper slowly, curling each piece around her fingertips before letting the warm wind blow it away. After that, she remembers, that tingle started in her toes and hands and she had to adjust her vision, like she imagined a crocodile did with his lids. She could hear everything, taste the colours of the sky, the grass, the dirt on the hill. She knew now that something had changed. That she had changed. That she had altered. Girls ran around her like she was not there. She could see the tops of their heads as they chased each other and sat together on this hill. She remembers. They smelled like soap.

The next day the Sisters sent her home with a note for her aunt, telling her that "her charge" had been absent from school without excuse the previous afternoon. Bernice recalls being livid (possessing the outrage of a teenager wronged by adults) and explaining that she *was* in class, and getting lectured about the ills and evils of lying.

Bernice had taken the note home, but Auntie Val hadn't shown up for three days at that point. It had taken another week for the Pecker Palace manager to notice and three days more for him to call Social Services. Enjoying the quiet, Bernice had been surprised when the police came to the door with the tired social worker. Looking around at Pecker Palace, she tried not to feel relieved. Relief felt like disloyalty.

❦

When Bernice awakens? Unfurls? Un-changes? Rises? she can smell Christ's Academy on her skin. It's impossible, she knows, but she has been there. The line between im/possible is not as absolute as it once was. That there is an arbitrariness in the world that she never suspected existed takes a physical toll on her. She can feel that her hands are clenched in front of her and a grunt of agitation sits bridled in her chest. It is as though her body was waking her spirit up. She finds the space between them awkward.

She used to wake up to her mother's singing. Maggie Meetoos had the most amazing voice. Two days out of three she was as tone-deaf as a riveter. On the third day, though – oh the third day! – she had the voice of a seasoned blues mistress. As

Tracey Lindberg

well, her momma could turn anything into a torch song. Until she was seventeen, Bernice thought "How Much is that Doggy in the Window?" was a blues anthem. Maggie's deep timbre belied her diminutive size. At five feet tall and one hundred pounds, her daughter's size dwarfed her. If it wasn't for her voice and her fists when she drank, you would forget that those sounds came from her body.

"*She wore bluuuuuuuuuue vellllllllllllllvet . . .*" Bobby Vinton on 78. Bernice remembers things frying, meat mostly, in a sizzling frenzy on the stove. Her mom shuffling across the ripped linoleum effortlessly as she stirred this and flipped that. The morning noise was comforting to Bernice who, hunched over her journal at the kitchen table, felt the difference between the stove heat and the summer heat stealing in the back screen door.

Back Then, before Now, before the Academy and all that followed, she dreamed that she could smell odd things in the lodge and she wondered if this was normal. She thought she smelled olives, but a bit stronger. Well, she couldn't actually smell it, but she knew it smelled like that in there. Now, of course, she knows this is – well, her normal.

One day, when her mom still puttered, Bernice sat in the kitchen and asked her questions. She had patience then, and Maggie was sometimes lost in thought before she answered. In that, she and her bigdaughter were the same. They shared an alertness sharpened by long periods of silence and thoughtfulness. In years, in too few years, when Maggie started vanishing, Bernice would remember that the silences could also be rich and full.

"How did you meet Dad?" "Did you have any other boy-friends?" "Where did you go to school?" "Did *Moshom** and *Kohkom* take you visiting, too?"

Maggie fluttered and her thoughts landed lightly, with her pecking at the questions and laughing every so often. Bernice learns that her dad gave her mom a terrible perfume their first Christmas together that smelled like rotten grapefruit, that the first time she cooked him his favourite meal – kidneys – their house smelled like pee for three days, that Valene had a crush on Conway Twitty for years, and that her mom dated one man before Bernice's dad. Sometimes, it didn't matter what she asked, she just got happy answers.

"Where did Freda come from?" In her mind's eye, Bernice sees her mom stop and cock her head, done eating. As if she had heard a potential predator rustling in the bush.

It was five minutes, at least, before her mother answered. "Same as everyone else. From a mom and a dad." Maggie's coffee cup slipped a bit, slopping some liquid on the counter.

"Enough. I better get finished in here." She walked outside, carrying the laundry soap, seemed to remember herself, and headed to the washer and dryer in the basement.

Bernice went under the stairs to have some alone time. When she came upon her auntie, she was only momentarily disappointed to share her space.

"Grab me the scissors, Bernice." Auntie Val had motioned with her lips to the vanity/shelf screwed in beside the door, which held books, pens and the scissors.

While everyone knew that Bernice's room was off limits, it also served as a haven for Valene when she visited the

* Grandfather.

Tracey Lindberg

Meetoos family. Never quite satisfied with being reserve-adjacent, Auntie Val took it personally that the family was not allowed to live there.

Looking out the window from the bed while painting her toenails, she had pointed to the rez with her lips. "Don't know why you guys never got a house on the rez."

"Mom says we can't have one," Bernice had answered, sitting down to do her own nails and immediately smearing her toenail on her bedspread.

"Oh did she?" Auntie Val narrowed her lips, a considerable task when you thought of the size of them. "Be a lot more room for you guys at Little Loon," she told Bernice.

"Hey dreamy-eyes, how's your old auntie look now?"

In truth, Valene *was* a vision. A red velvet dress fought for supremacy over her stomach and wearily pledged its allegiance to her auntie's wide bottom. Her eyelashes, totally regrown since an unfortunate eyelash curler incident, fluttered prettily over amber brown eyes.

And her mouth, her singularly Cree mouth, which laughs so loud and curls up so easily, was bathed in a shade of red that only clowns and Valene Calliou can wear.

She had stared at her little mother, with the mammoth bosom and the truck driver mouth, the living proof that a fat Indian woman can get laid, and said, "Oh Auntie, you're a dream." And meant it.

For Bernice Meetoos had no doubt that sort of woman, her sort of woman, could be loved. She herself had seen the glowworm in the eyes of a few men. Mostly they were older, sometimes they were drunk, and often they went home alone. But they were out there. Out there waiting for this gorgeous smart big woman to finally enjoyably, consensually and delightfully screw them.

Auntie Val, Bernice had no doubt, had all of this and knew it to be true.

"She's spending too much time with *your* sister," her uncle Larry had told Bernice's mom, his oldest sister, one night as Bernice stood listening outside the kitchen window.

She can and did imagine her mom wiping her hands on her dishtowel and brushing her hair from her eyes. Now, Bernice thinks of them as tear-stained eyes, but then she just knew her mom to be exhausted. From taking care. From propping up. From being the one.

"She's your sister, too. And it seems to me, Larry," she said in her soft drone, "Bernice needs someone to lead her."

"But that old –"

Impatience cloaks her words. "Enough."

For a while after that she avoided her mother's eyes. Sometimes it was hard to look at her mom, her mom in the size four dress, and remember that they were related. And that she could not follow her.

❧

Bernice squeezes her eyes shut and tries not to think of that feeling. Of near home. There. Her mom.

It seems to her that she has been running on a half a tank since she moved to the ocean. She never thought that she would live near the ocean. Sure, she watched *The Beachcombers* and wondered about the life Jesse would have outside of Molly's Reach. Like if he moved to Vancouver or something. She went straight to Edmonton when she left the San. She found it changed since she had lived there last. The Academy had turned co-ed. The neighbourhood feel was gone. What she had liked about the city best when she lived there and was looking forward to upon her return was the anonymity. It still existed, that *something* about its size and the feeling you get when no one knows you in such a big place. She had liked seeing hundreds of new people and not having a past or a future with them. Walking down Jasper Avenue, perched between rich and poor, its split personality like a memory or a premonition of something unpredictable. Sometimes, just to scare herself, she would lose track of where she walked and would be just like a baby in the middle of some huge shopping mall. Except, no one was looking for her. When she left her auntie's house the day after the change with deer fur still on her pants, she knew she would not live there ever again. She was done, it was too close to home, and she didn't want to remember. Those memories littered her mind like a sandstorm.

In the city, you could smell earth, but it was the disposable and compostable earth (mould, mildew and dust) that she found suffused her clothes, her hair and the stuff she carried in her cart. The smellmemory competes with the yeasty richness of the bakery and she feels it in the room. Her home. Her old home. Her notional home. Living in Edmonton, around Edmonton, about Edmonton, under Edmonton was the same as living in and about the rez. Living next to the reserve in a house at the outskirts of town was no different than living under the pedestrian bridge next to the Kinsmen Centre. There were woods, a river, she didn't fit in, and she had to rely on herself for protection.

It was a life she chose, or that chose her, once she was in the city. When her auntie lost her job. When she was left alone. She was old enough. After the Academy, care, and when she came back to Edmonton before the San, she made her way just fine – for a long time she appreciated and lived off the goodwill of friends, then friends of friends, and eventually strangers. Inevitably, when the goodwill ran out, so did she. Much of that time is perfectly clear in her head. She had moments of perfection living on the streets. Philosophical discussions, arguments about Indian rights, and exchanges about the old ways and how to live them in a new time. Of course, those were tempered by lost times. Times that are not so perfectly clear, even with the clarity she seems to possess on the Sealy, where she was flanked by harsh words, cruelties and fights. Then, she escaped and changed herself. She has little memory of Then, but when she came back from wherever her spirit spirited her she liked to imagine she was a wolf, living in the green and watching the city through wolf eyes. Until one night. She didn't know how long she had been gone before she slept. Didn't know how long she slept.

The next morning. She had a crow feather between her lips when she woke up.

When she allows herself to think of the past, it is a past that was safe and from which she had taken pieces to construct a manageable present. Most often, she thinks of who she was then in terms of what she could see and smell around her.

There is a cacophonous noise in the bakery below her. She can hear Lola enjoying the busy work of preparation. Thump thump thump. Murmur. Dull thud dull thud dull thud. Laugh. Bernice imagines she can smell yeast and butter in the waves of rising heat. The ovens make a low hummmm and ground the cooking in something solid and permanent.

"Can you imagine?" Lola cackles, and a new cadence answers. Chops and softens, rises and lilts, with no discernible word pattern. For some reason, Bernice is struck with a thought: that sounds happy.

True, she has the smell of loss on her and is anxious in her demeanour and stares too long but she knows this feeling.

She can feel Freda's bones, tired and sad, curving so much like her own, below her.

acimowin

Crow sat down and lit herself a cigarette.
She had flown an awfully long way and she neededwanted a cigarette.
So she
had one.
Crow had come a long way to learn big words and to make her voice
more beautiful. No one told Crow a crow is always a crow, and that
their voices would always be
an undignified cawwww!

She had decided that she wanted
a certain lifestyle, as many crows do,
and that she was willing to transform herself to do it. Crow had
learned a good trick,
Crow could make herself beautiful and pleasant.
When she wanted to, Crow could look sleek and exotic.
Crow looked at herself in the mirror
and she liked what she saw.
She had sleek black feathers, the blackest of eyes, and a lean long
shape.
Crow thought that it was a pity that not everyone could experience
her beauty.
A pity, but a blessing!
She, Crow, cawlaughed to herself.
Crow wore the tightest and most revealing of outfits.
If it was backless, sleeveless, sheer, high cut, and black Crow would
pour herself into it and out of it to please her many admirers.
She was not blessed with thick,
luxurious feathers but she had learned tricks to make them look thick.

No one told Crow that a scavenger's breath always smells like death.

pawatamowin

In that dream, then, she has written in someone else's hand:

Muskeg
Lavender
Gelatin

Beneath it, in her own:
Stop.

Tracey Lindberg

Then. She remembers Then. Her body steel. Her mind closed. She does not feel changed. She feels afraid. Wants Lola or Freda to come up. To stop this one.

She had woken up. This time. In a room. That was clearly. Not her home.

She woke up.

In a room.

And could not move.

She woke up.

In a room.

And was tied to herself.

She woke up.

In a room.

And was herself tied.

She woke up.

In a room.

And found.

She was not changed.

She woke up.

In a room.
And learned.
She was crazy.

6

NOWHERE

anisinowin: lost. the act of losing one's way or being lost

I T SEEMED, WHEN THEY FOUND HER, that Bernice was
sleeping in a dumpster behind a Lebanese place on Whyte
Avenue. She had been in the city for years at that point, having
left the Ingelsons' foster home so long before. One year inter-
wove and wrapped around another. The owners of the place
had seen her there upon occasion but had decided to let her
sleep. After a while, when they thought she had not changed
position for some time (if they only knew), the owners called
the fire department. That they should do this, instead of calling the police, was understandable. Homeless people, in fact
an Indian woman (or, that's what they called her in the paper),
had been set on fire in their dumpsters before (and, really, to
think Bernice oblivious to that fact was to seriously misinter-
pret her circumstance).

However, officials are officials and they took Bernice and put her in a late-arriving ambulance, the attendants clearly disappointed (That she was not in pain? That she was alive? That she appeared to be the indigent Indigenous?). She had no idea how long ago they took her from that dumpster. It had been her sometimes home since she ran from the Ingelsons'. Years. Four? Five? She was pissed after being rustled out of it, angry at the police, and then enraged at the attendants. And. Then. She skipped. She skipped ahead to this place – no idea how long she had been here within the cheerless minty green walls, no idea how long she has been wearing the hospital gown and robe she was wearing (by the smell of it, not too long). Or where those moccasins came from. There, in the San (Alberta Regional Psychiatric Services – formerly "The Sanatorium"), she led a quiet life. Read books. Thought. Seldom spoke. And. Every so often. Went under. Shifted. It was not like Now, Now being so intertwined with Then that her heartbeat seems not to be within her and her senses are alive to Then more than Now. Thinkdreaming of the San, she knows that she developed something. Something like cognizance. A sort of stormy harmony. Where licking flames coexisted with the coolness of metal. Words with noiselessness. Freedom within a straitjacket.

If she could have seen outside of herself then, she would have seen the stream of doctors and nurses who walked by her each day. When she first got there, still crusty wounds and all, she was open as a window – smiling and talking. If she was asked something that she did not want to answer, she would smile and await the next question. Eventually, she was left to her own devices, and didn't have to talk to anyone anymore. She preferred it that way. Happiest when she is alone, Bernice wore her need for quiet like a veil. What she found was that the ritual of that place, or the ceremony if you will, was soothing in its repetition. The San was no safer than living outside in Edmonton, no more peaceful than the house she had to share with dangerous uncles. In fact, the hospital was in some ways much more dangerous. The caw caw caw crowing of madwomen and madmen ruptures the silence around her, perforating quiet, gaining space and fading away. That noise had disturbed her then and it antagonizes her now. If Freda or Lola were in the room, they might see her brow set and lips pursed; toughened and ready for fight. She knew, though, that in that place there was ceremony all around her, and that within that she had padded her home at the San. She washed her hands four times, repeated certain words (peace peace peace peace) (mother mother mother mother) four times, and patted herself four times (bless yourself, bless yourself, bless yourself, bless yourself). And late at night, when the inmates truly went wild and when she thought of Loon and found herself agitated, she let the pain burn up, the ashwords falling around her in groups of four.

As days rubbed the edges of the nights smooth, Bernice would find that time danced around her, sidestepping bedpans and sashaying by orderlies. Always forward, but sometimes it was a jingle dance – pronounced and melodic. Some months would pass like a traditional dancer's dance at a pow wow, slow and steady, even and smooth. One whole year disappeared like a fancy dance – you had to watch real careful before it was gone. And Bernice would smile, and talk, sleep, sit quiet and wait. She wasn't looking for an opportune time to escape or anything like that. And it's not that she trusted the San staff to tell her when she was "better." With the same acute sense that told her when to shift, Bernice knew when she was done. With a place. It was when she ignored that voice that told her she was finished that she got into trouble. Who would she have been if there had been more women in the house than men that night? What would have happened if her dad had not left for good with Terry Badger (well, with Terry Badger, eventually he found another Terry-like woman, and another)?

Her blood bubbles and her head swoons a bit. She is tired. Waiting. Tired of waiting. And feels. Her pillow. Wet with tears.

7

WHO WILL LOVE YOU

awîyak ka kehnipat: someone who slept

pawatamowin
dirt.

BERNICE FINDS HERSELF ANNOYED BY LOLA. Lola of the lovely meals, Lola of the cooing that doesn't sound right coming from her mouth, Lola of the language she can't quite understand. Her skin, desensitized and disassociated with herself for so long, feels alive even while she is motionless under the nubby and starting-to-smell-like-damp-moss pink sheet. The flow of memories washes over her like the cold water washes over a stone during spring runoff. She feels unafraid to sleep for the first time in her adult life. Also. For the first time. She comes to understand that "Cross your heart and hope to die" is an oath, not a prayer, and she has stopped saying it before she goes to sleep.

She is so hungry. Not for food, not for drink, not for foreign skin. This appetite that sits next to her now is relatively unknown and persistent. She is hungry for family. For the women she loves. For the sounds of her language. For the peace of no introduction, no backstory, no explanation. She misses her aunties, her cousins and her mom. She thinks that she maybe misses who her dad was, too, but isn't sure. She wouldn't know what that felt like. She misses the Cree sense of humour. She misses her Auntie Val. Misses the production of her auntie getting ready.

"I dunno why these fundamentalists have to look at a guy to know that he's dead," Auntie Val had frowned to herself, and anyone who was within earshot of the bathroom mirror, one hot summer years ago on the rez. She had been trimming her hair, actually evening it out, for well over an hour.

"There!" she had pronounced, standing back and swinging her head back and forth at Bernice.

Tracey Lindberg

"How do I look? No, move and let me see, honey."

She pushed Bernice out of her way, put her hands on her hips and said, "I look just like that big girl that Madonna hangs around with."

"You mean Rosie O'Donnell?"

Wow. Valene didn't watch television or go to movies. She looked closely at her auntie.

"Kind of, I guess," she lied.

"Thought so." She paused for a second. "Crazy Marie used to do their makeup at the funeral home in Lac La Biche."

She didn't pause or wait for discussion, pulled on lamé sandals, oblivious to the rules of fashion. Val knew no one noticed her feet, and it was a shame, too. Valene's feet are quite thick and heavy feet, corns and calluses everywhere, earth where there should be none, and grass stains where brown skin should prevail. They are beautiful and decrepit, animal and lifefull. Too used and too magnificent to peek out from under slacks or long skirts like those stuck-in-a-cave-too-long feet that skinny girls have.

"Did they feel, I don't know, strange?" Bernice summons that moment again and recalls that she had felt no revulsion, just disjointedness between body and spirit.

"A job's a job, Birdie. No one does anything like that for free, I bet." She started to paint her fingernails a bright pink.

The talk soon returned to the funeral Bernice had attended the day before.

"Did you get to see Blanche's girls?" Auntie Val asked, eyeliner-encased sad eyes momentarily flicking in her direction.

"Only for a second, Winona had Bad Boy with her – do

you know when he was in B.C. he threw a butt out near *Pima-tisewin?*"

"Hhhhmph." Her auntie never tore anyone down. "And Winona is such a pretty girl." She pinned her dark hair up on her head and sucked in her cheeks.

"How did it look?"

She and her auntie often checked the progress of the tree, in the same way many people spoke quietly of a sacred white buffalo born in the States. Bernice thought a minute before speaking.

"It looked okay, the leaves maybe looked a little brown, but it's not like everybody's saying. I don't know what the big deal is."

"Oops, I dropped some of that hair goop on your mom's carpet." Val wiped it with her toe and pushed it into the rug.

"It's okay, leave it." Bernice watched as her auntie ignored her and bustled out from Bernice's under-the-stair room to the kitchen to get a cloth. She was surprisingly fast for a big woman and in no time at all was back and dabbing at the rug.

Bernice took the hair gel from her auntie, sat her on the bed and began to pin piles of curls on her head, carefully massaging the gel onto each piece of hair. They sat together for a half-hour, wordless, enjoying the radio and each other's company. Val put on her outfit – a lilac satin pantsuit cinched at the waist, part of what she calls her "Saan Store Sexy" collection. A horn honked outside. Her auntie hugged her warmly and kissed her, leaving a trace of "Ever So Peachy" on her cheek.

"Don't wait up, eh? Might be someone's lucky night!"

Tracey Lindberg

She had winked and sashayed down the hall, slamming the front door and teetering, Bernice had imagined, all the way to Vince Thunderchild's pickup truck.

And. Now. Thinking. About Then. Her senses dance in the little room above the bakery. She can smell her, all of her – from her moosehide moccasins to her Chanel No. 5 knock-off perfume. She smells the wild and the womanly; fullness and ferocity of her little mother. She thinks she may have shifted and memory brought her auntie into the room, for she can sense her.

Auntie Val filled the room, fought the light for brilliance in her mind. And. Now. Stands, waiting, over her favourite niece. Bernice's skin flushes, her stomach growls and a small vein on the left side of her forehead pulses. In her state of near-consciousness and semi-alertness, she thinks she hears a ghost from Then Now. "Well, looky here!" says a familiar voice in the unfamiliar room at the top of the stairs. "My gosh, Bernice, you are a *shallow* of your former self!"

Auntie Val has come at last.

❧

In the gentle space between wake and sleep, Bernice knows that those three downstairs are stewing in something, trying to come up with a plan. If she could speak, if she still had English, she would tell them to just leave her be. To find her family and bring them to Gibsons. To find that Frugal Gourmet and get him to tell them his secrets. To dreambake and dreamcook. To find her aunties and bring them to her.

She cannot look at Auntie Val. In her head, she yells at her to keep it down and warns her not to talk to her during the Frugal Gourmet's third show of the day. "I'm going to miss my show," she hisses inside.

Her auntie points at the TV with her lips and talks to Bernice without speaking.

"Your show? It's some cookin' show. The same cookin' show that you watch every day in your torn pants and stinky pyjamas." She creates a space for herself on the mattress, which no one else would dare to do, by shifting her buttocks left and right until she is seated next to Bernice.

"Birdie, Bernice honey, what's goin' on? Are you all right?"

She tells Auntie to get out and memorizes one cup of mayonnaise and a teaspoon of lemon juice. It won't be until later, after her ceremony, after her brain/some spirit summons these ingredients weeks from now, that she will remember her meanness. Still, even though she feels bad she feels it in a detached way. Sort of like a photograph of what her nastiness looks like in the distance.

She smells her leave: the scent of grief and fear. Bernice waits until her auntie leaves the room after sitting with her for an hour or so, staring at her, to throw a shaky hand over her mouth, and cry into it.

꒐꒐

Seconds, minutes, hours, days later.

"Do you remember," Auntie Val looks for the word and then snaps her eyes at Bernice, "sleepwalking sometimes?"

Tracey Lindberg

Bernice flinches, which Freda might miss while picking at her cuticles, but which she fears her aunt will know is her inside trying to get out.

"Yep, seems to me that this isn't the first time I seen this."

Bernice captures the thoughtwords her aunt is sending her. She sees herself sitting under the stairs, for days on end. Drunken parties that went on endlessly overhead. Crying. Screaming. Yelling. Sometimes it was Freda. But mostly it was Everybody Else. Everybody Else punching (a little of the old Indian lovin'), guzzling, dancing. Laughing, crying, screaming, wheedling, feeling, touching, kneeling, creeping. Like they were trying to get to white man's hell faster just to prove the point.

And she sees herself: little Bernice, medium Bernice and Big Bernice lying on her bed, staring straight up. Wishing herself anywhere. But. There.

Her auntie stares at her for what seems like hours. Bernice makes herself more still than she has been in all of the days since she "took to her sickbed" (as she had overheard Lola telling the Whippets). She knows it is not the silence that will worry Val. No, she has been silent since she was a teenager. Something else. Her auntie will notice something else. Missing. From her eyes. From her spirit. Bernice saw it in her mom and she saw it in the uncles. She is afraid her auntie will notice what is missing, not what is happening.

Bernice can hear her auntie's thoughts; they come out cautiously into the room like a lynx leaving the treeline. She knows her little mother wants to tell her about her mom, about Maggie at the end. Bernice can feel the warmth of her auntie and how much she wants to touch her. She lets the thoughts hang there for a second and then wills them to the floor with a thud. *Your mom did what she had to do, Bernice, she was sorry for everything, and before she left she told me that she loved her girl Birdie best.* The words rush out. Bernice wills them to drop.

She blocks her auntie's thoughts. Remembers Val telling her that she had always regretted not learning the medicines from her *kohkom*; she wonders if her auntie thinks *Kohkom* (they called her a witch, but as the sisters grew older came to understand that everything had a good side and a bad side) could have done something about – this. This being her, all skinnied up and shaking in what appears to be sleep.

Kohkom Rose would have taken care of business all right, Val thinks, and slips that one by Bernice.

Bernice waits her out. Wills her out. Thinks her out.

Come to think of it, Val thinks at her, *the old lady probably would have loved that crazy chef that you are so obsessed with. That guy knows something about herbs, spices and food magic.*

Her auntie's stomach grumbles delightedly with the smell of pie wafting up the stairs. Bernice feels her take a long look at her and hears her being sure to carefully step quietly in her moccasins as she makes her way down the stairs to see Lola and Freda.

LOLA

"Who keeps playing that frigging music?" Lola says, cigarette in lips and full house in hands.

Tracey Lindberg

She and the Whippets are on the fourth hour of their weekly poker game and she is always grumpy when she has a good hand. Whippet One folds when she hears Lola's tone.

"Who?" Whippet One asks her, delicately skewering an olive with the one-inch nail on the pinky of her left hand.

"You heard me, who's playing it, fer chrissakes?" Lola growls. This time, Whippet Four hears the anger in her voice and folds as well.

"The band, there's some sort of . . . band or kids playing the drums and howling. Sounds like something from that party the Indians throw each year," Whippet Two, oblivious to the vocal signal (after all, she's only been coming to the game for two years), snaps in response, pressing her cards together in a tight near-pile, so that only the numbers are visible.

"I hate that crap," Lola mutters, throwing more chips (about two dollars' worth – they have a ten-dollar limit per hand) onto the green felt table set up in the front window of the bakery.

"It's been playing day and night at full volume for two and a half weeks now," she squeals, tossing her cards down and scooping the pot with bangled, tanned and leathery arms.

Deals another hand. Lights another smoke. "Party? No, I think it's a . . ." – she searches for the right word and lowers her voice (she also lowers her voice when discussing things that are foreign to her, among them: Africa, Native and the word *black*) – ". . . a wow wow. I don't get these kids today."

The Whippets all murmur their assent. The Kids Today are a frequent topic of discussion at their weekly games. And their weekly pub hop. And their daily coffee talks. The Whippets, a peculiarly uniform group of sixty-year-old skinny women from across Canada, found each other because they all suntanned at the same beach back in 1982. All but Lola divorced and smokers, they have a lot to talk about. In '82, though, they still considered themselves The Kids of Today. But Whippet Three's hysterectomy, menopause and Lola's on again, off again AA meetings have forced them to recognize the unrecognizable: Time owns you. You don't own it.

"I can't hear anything," Whippet Three says. She was not the sharpest knife in the drawer, anyhow, but it still seems odd to Lola.

"What? Listen closely, dear." Spearing a baby dill with her ever-present toothpick, Lola wills her to hear it.

"Umm. I think it's a pow wow." Whippet Four is never comfortable pointing out the obvious.

"Spit it out, Jaysus, Margo, you'd think you just learned to talk," Lola bites at her.

Margo folds. "Pow wow. I think it's called a pow wow. And I don't hear anything, either, Lo'."

"Damned if I'm not going penile," she hisses in Whippet Lingo. They all laugh at the oft-repeated joke.

Whippet One folds.

"Or maybe that's catching." Whippet Three points to the roof of the bakery, Bernice's floor.

Lola looks around quickly to see if the girl's relations are nearby and then slowly and deliberately stares hard at all of the Whippets, most of them avoiding her gaze. Whippet Three does not. She is not particularly fond of Whippet Three (who replaced the original Whippet Three who did not fight a valiant fight against pancreatic cancer).

"You watch your damn mouth, Missus," Lola orders her, thumping the heel of her hand on the counter.

The floor overhead creaks and Lola stands up, ear cocked.

The familiar clatter of cheap plastic heels on hardwood clack clack clack overhead.

"It's that damn cousin of hers." She throws her hand in, in what looks like disgust but which is not.

"How long is she staying, Lola?" Whippet Two asks not-so-innocently, stoking the fire. Whippet Two has not done anything innocently since she was a pre-teenager.

Lola busies herself getting beers for everyone from the cooler. "As long as she needs to, I suppose." She clearly enunciates every word.

"That aunt of hers came with enough luggage to move in," Whippet Two snipes.

None of the Whippets understands the softness of Lola's heart and the feelings of kindness that she has for Bernice. Lola has thought about that and tries to convince herself that she thinks of The Kid the same way she thinks of those homeless people around the corner. With embarrassment that she has while they do not. Not that she thinks Bernice would even want any of her stuff. No, that desire is quite below The Kid. Nope, the stuff that Lola has that she is aware and embarrassed of in front of Bernice is right in this room. Friends, conversation, peace of mind. She feels tenderness for the girl because she suspects no one has been tender to her before.

On those nights when Bernice teetered awkwardly on heels down the stairs, and to godknowswhere, Lola could not sleep until she came home. And egads, when she came home.

Bruised. Bloodied. Empty. Those scars on her arms and hands lookin' like they want to jump out from underneath the skin. They look like burns, and Lola wonders what and when. It just broke her heart.

She is a reminder to Lola that she herself used to be with rough men, too. That she used to have those same black eyes, same torn lips and same bloodied teeth. *But only with one man,* she reminds herself. Yep, this was a completely different kettle of fish. It is almost like The Kid is *going out to get beat up.* And that is impossible.

When the Whippets leave, she treats herself to the last of the cold cuts, cheeses and assorted pickled vegetables. She no longer goes to a great deal of trouble on poker nights. When they first started the Whippet Club, the Wednesday night poker club, the Whippets would exercise their culinary one-upmanship and prepare feasts of dainties, finger foods and banquet offerings. As time went by, the feasts became less lavish, and now they all order deli trays from Sal's Sausage Emporium.

They have also developed a conversational shorthand, in the way that old friends do together. It wasn't until their twelfth year that they got tipsy and renamed body parts and functions. Twelve years to come up with "hoo ha" and "dry heave."

Nope, she does not love the Whippets. She sees their cruelty and deplores the mirror image in herself. And the way she looks when she sees her reflection in how Bernice looks at her. Looked at her. It moves her. A different woman. A different Lola. Quiet kindness and soft intelligence meets harsh observations and boiling wit. She is a patchwork quilt made up of

Tracey Lindberg

who she would have been. If her life had turned out differently.

Lola has never had any children herself and cannot imagine what motherly feelings are like. Still, The Kid touches on a place that she had forgotten existed.

She lights a smoke, still picking her teeth with the toothpick, and stares at the streetlights outside of the bakery.

The Kid is dying, she thinks, and rejects the notion almost as quickly as she thought it. If she is dying, Bernice was doing it before she got to Gibsons. Until her aunt got there, she and Freda had noticed there was still a spark in The Kid. A look in her eyes some days, a look in her eyes that reminded Lola of something familiar and too painful to call up. But she recognized and knows it, and sees it in that mirror.

And no matter what that look betrays, Lola also sees something in her that reflects in both of their mirrors. Survivor.

When Lola first moved to Gibsons from Biggs, California ("Just two hours off route 99!" went the jingle), she didn't have this, this coating on her. Of harshness, of weatheredness, of having felt. But that was two near-husbands, six jobs and countless lovers ago. She felt old at eighteen. But she was still kind.

In her youth, she had been a stunner. Petite and athletic, without all of the Whippetishness that yo-yo dieting, a pack of Carltons a day and the fevered California sun can have on a person. She felt more. She gambled more. She was on the run, she always told the Whippets, but in truth she was not being chased but was chasing. Something. Anything out of the Biggs, California ordinary. And when you are attractive and chasing in Vancouver, eventually you get caught yourself.

She was caught by Stanley Manklow. A completely beautiful specimen of a man. She hadn't learned to read tarot cards or mean eyes yet. And both would have told her more than she wanted to know about Stan Manklow. Oh, he had been good at first. Flowers, little notes and secret caressing touches when she wasn't expecting them. The thought of those days still left her a bit breathless. Or maybe it's the Carltons. But he had a way. "The touch," her mom called it. Yep, he had the touch with women, generally. More particularly, he could drive Lola completely crazy with desire.

It wasn't the last time she would learn the lesson about gifts in bright shiny packages.

How she had loved him. And oh, how he loved. It started out innocently enough. After they had been married for a few weeks, he was a little rough in his lovemaking. By the second month he was pushing and prodding in a way that was foreign to her. Not one to play the dutiful wife, she began to fight back.

It wasn't until years later that she knew he was hitting her for that. He wanted a submissive woman in the bedroom, didn't really care who was boss outside of it, and he was going to make her one, dammit.

After her fourth trip to the emergency ward, her dad and her brother drove up to Vancouver just to beat the living hell out of Stan so he would know what brutality felt like. She kept his stuff so he would come back, but he never did. Later, she heard from one of the Whippets that he had become a born-again Christian or something.

"Figgers," she mutters. And it really does. It figures that he had to turn to God to get that demon out of him. It figures that he would think that all was forgiven. That the bruises, which he never had but enjoyed raising, had healed. And the ironic thing was that after he left her, for a time she became the subservient woman that he was looking to create.

Two relationships later, and the physical violence started again. She wondered, wonders, if there is something about her that inspires this. Invites this. She didn't have her dad to beat the hell out of him the next time. The next time, she did it herself. And found herself pleased at the power she possessed. This next time she left, both Vancouver and the Vancouver man (the quintessential Vancouver man and city councillor, as it turned out). Whenever he runs for re-election, and he always runs and he always wins, she scribbles "Woman Hater" on his posters over his doughy family photo.

She hears the heavy clumping of Val's moccasin-clad feet and then the tick tick tickiness of Skinny Freda's heels above her.

Probably scratching the hell outta my hardwoods with those damn boots of hers, she thinks, unkindly. But still, something in her has warmed to the Indian version of herself, if only because she is so close to The Kid. She thinks about inviting Freda down for coffee, and of course the aunt, but the room is too full tonight, what with her ghosts and all.

That skinny one keeps looking at her. Big smile that doesn't flower in her eyes, pulled lips around square teeth. When she isn't looking, Lola sees a little collapse in her, like the air popped out when no one was looking. And if she ever ate, Lola had yet to see it. One day when she reached for the coffeepot – that thing had never worked as hard as when Freda showed up at the bakery (tiny skirt, big sweater and tottering on heels like a girl going to her first dance) – Lola spotted a rash of scars from her wrist to the last visible space below her elbow. Sensing the old woman's eyes on her, Freda quickly adjusted her sleeve and made a joke about drinking one cup and paying three. From then on, Lola could never get a look because the girl wore that great big blue sweater over everything – even in the heat of the morning when the ovens made the kitchen fiercely warm.

Until the Big One got there, Lola thought the chatter and small talk was going to drive her mad. *That woman could talk the ear off a goat,* she thinks. She, herself a nervous talker, realizes she has nothing on Bernice's tiny cousin.

That is one thing that strikes her as strange about Freda. She is, to anyone's read, almost waiflike. But, Lola thinks she fills each room she comes into, what with her stream-of-consciousness nattering, fidgeting and constant alertness. It's something else, though, she thinks. She is bigger than her body. The thought is both lovely and uncomfortable to Lola.

Watching her enter the kitchen, head to the carafe and take an ever-present cup of coffee with her, Lola's eyes trail Freda as she makes her way up to Bernice's apartment. There is no noise from up there, all three of the women seem to be sharing the space with silence. However, Lola could swear that the upstairs is filled with communication that sometimes slips down the stairwell, pauses at the kitchen and lands around her.

No, she tells herself. Such things are impossible.

But, she makes a promise to herself and to The Kid that she will find out what is going on in there. All in good time.

Tracey Lindberg

AUNTIE VAL

Today Val nodded at Bernice and she thinks she caught her niece about to nod back. Val is not one to fool with, and even though she feels Go Away! Go Away! Go Away! emanating from Bernice, she takes no offence. Valene catches it all and files it away with other things dear to her.

Bernice, to Val's eye, looks to be sleeping, but she knows better. She knows that needing to dream this much meant that Bernice was communicating with spirits. Val welcomes those spirits by smudging every day and by leaving food out for them with each meal. That little moniaskwew*monia*downstairs has not said a word about it – every shared meal portioned equally four times, and Valene taking the first one out the door. She knows from this that Bernice's boss is either kind or lacking curiosity.

She also knows that she will never again let anyone make Bernice do anything she doesn't want to do. So, since she seems to want to sleep, Auntie Val lets her sleep. Freda and Lola have long since stopped objecting to this – maybe skinny people's organs are so close to the skin that their feelings are desensitized, she thinks – and they let her sleep now, too. While Bernice sleeps, her auntie slathers bear grease on her scars, as though she can heal the years-old damage. Bernice does not respond but she does not shift an inch (which she will do if Freda is making too much noise or rambling on too long), so Valene takes this to mean her niece is comfortable with the application of the medicine.

Bernice also seems to like that little weird cook on the TV, so Auntie Val puts that on three times a day. Thank heavens for the CBC and Canadian content, she thinks. No matter what her state before the show – moaning, thrashing, snoring or peacefully resting – when that man comes on Bernice is rapt (as rapt as you can be with your eyes closed) with attention. Years later, she will remember an added detail that had escaped her; Valene could feel impatience in the room after the show ended. She would also construct that she heard shuffling upstairs after she went to the kitchen, but in her heart she knows that is not true. What she does know for sure is that she leaves as soon as the show is on and that when she returns later there is a feeling of accomplishment or business in the room.

Sure, it took time to get the schedule down, but they seem to have made a peaceful place. Not like the first day when they yelled at each other, mouths closed and eyes flashing (two open and two closed). Maybe it was the shock of seeing Bernice skinny, with flesh hanging on her, that scared her enough to yell. Maybe she wanted to yell until Bernice opened her eyes. Whatever the reason, they did not yell now. They don't speak and they don't quietspeak. Sometimes, though, she can feel an electric buzz of awareness, of live voice or spirit and maybe of needing to communicate from her niece. When she feels that, she pulls her chair closer and hums to her, singing old songs, pow wow 69ers and some show tune that she can't get out of her head. Other times, when she feels that buzz, she will just hug Bernice or pat her hand.

It feels insignificant in the scope of things, with her there, peeing on the sly (no one knows when she goes), eating a handful of this and a handful of that. Still, she can't really measure the value of being able, having to touch someone, let alone what it is like to need to be touched with love.

Mostly, Valene thinks that Bernice is tired. She believes her niece doesn't want to have to talk, to answer, to be a part of some time when she needs to think. Val imagines she is afraid that if she opens her mouth she will let out those little parts, like atoms or some parts of her that are forming the new her. Like, if she thought that if she mixed them up by talking or paying attention, or even by moving too fast, that new her would be stuck where it is Now. Valene won't let that happen. In her mind, she likens it to being knocked up – you have to lay off the booze and smokes until the baby is ready to come out. Only this time it was talking and joking Birdie has to avoid. She wants everyone to let her just be – and be quiet until the time is right. She is not ready yet.

Freda and Lola disappear for hours, clatter around in their heels and have periods that feel remarkably like silence around each other. Val knows herself well enough to know that she will not let up. She sits near Bernice and hums the old songs, does beading on the bed beside her, cleans her up and has full conversations with her.

"You know, my girl," she says to her one afternoon, "you didn't have to disappear when I went . . . away. Could'a . . ." But even the extraordinarily resourceful woman doesn't have the words to describe where she had gone or why. "I heard about you, you know. Looked out for you when you lived . . . in Edmonton. On your own." Valene can't bring herself to mention that she, herself, went mad with worry when Bernice's visits stopped. She struggles to tell her niece about the nights she wandered in and out of the bars downtown, asked about Bernice at shelters and walked the paths of the ravine. That she felt relief when she heard she went to Loon and even when she went to the San. Both were preferable to . . . what she could never talk about.

"One night I thought, I could'a sworn I felt you . . . your presence. I was under the bridge near the Kinsmen and I *smelled* you," Valene continues, "I looked and looked but all I saw was a mangy old coyote and an *oho.**" Chuckling, she remembers that coyote staring at her, panting from the heat, sitting there like she owned the world.

She busies herself tidying, swears those steady staring-straight-ahead eyes – when they are open (which is becoming less and less frequent when Val is around) – on her look just like that mangy old thing, and she also thinks she sees something akin to panic or anxiety in those eyes before they snap shut when she opens the closet. She organizes the shoes and slippers on the floor, hangs up a clean uniform and then comes upon a file folder stashed behind the Aer Lingus bag.

It feels warm, almost hot, to her touch and she does not want to open it. She carries part of the file downstairs with her so she can get her reading glasses from her purse.

Case file: AB-IA23546-444 *Meetoos, Bernice Clara*

June 22, 2xxx. 22 year old Native woman admitted at 15:30 via ambulance with partial thickness burns noted to arms and

---

* Owl.

Tracey Lindberg

legs bilaterally. Feet and hands severely burnt – potentially full thickness burns on heels and fingertips. 5 inch burns on arms. .5-1 inch burns on fingers and toes. 3 inch burns on heels. IV N/S established in right arm. Given Morphine 5 mg IV push, for pain management @ 1540 hours and Ativan 2 mg SL for agitation.

Patient involved in a fire that killed her uncle and injured the patient. Remains severely agitated – yelling. Consult sent to psych. Pt. was lone survivor. Sat with Pt. half hour with no response. Made therapeutic group session mandatory for next week. Personal sess. booked daily with Dr. Maria Carver.

Patient is Native woman. Obese.

Auntie Val listens for her niece, and turns the page. How had she gotten her medical record from the San? she wonders. Bernice had it rolled up and bunched with her diary and those stupid *Tiger Beat* pictures. She reads it, over and over, holding back her anger and feeling it convert to tears.

"*Kicimakanes,*"* she whispers.

She has felt this pity before, but never so intensely and certainly not for someone who had done such a *thing*. And, although she has willed them apart for years, the pieces rain down, come together, and she thinks she may fall apart. Because in her heart she now knows. Bernice killed someone. She has always thought of it as an accident because the truth was too painful to even admit to herself. Now, she knows, is the time for truth. She is so engrossed, and feels pitiable herself,

---

* Poor gal, a pitiful person.

that she is largely unaware of her environment. She knows she is alone, those two skinny soul sisters having taken off for the evening. Some sound breaks through her thoughts and she hears something above her; she can't be sure, but it sounded like a footstep. She girthily strides upstairs and is shocked when she walks into the bedroom. Bernice is not there. She checks the closet. Nothing. Hears a faucet drip and walks to the bathroom. She hadn't bothered to take off Bernice's uniform and was surprised to see that Bernice was nude and sitting in the grey water, with bubbles all around her and her hair washed. She sat still as a rock, but Val isn't fooled, this stuff didn't happen by magic.

"Well, looky, looky," Val says, mad that her niece was mobile and able while seemingly unwilling to get out of bed. "Someone musta thought she smelled bad enough to want to get out of those clothes!"

Bernice does not respond.

"You're not foolin' me, Bernice," she says forcefully.

Bernice's left eye twitches.

"If you think I am pulling you out of there, you are crazier than I thought." Val stands, hands on hips, expectant. When Bernice remains in the water, she turns her back, and says, "I won't even look, just get up and get dressed. You see? I got your pyjamas set out for you already."

When she hears no noise, she storms to the living room, grabs the rest of the file folder and nearly races back to the bathroom. "I'm gonna sit down and read all of this – all of your stuff – until you decide to get outta that tub and get dressed," she threatens.

Bernice remains in the tub.

"Stubborn, stubborn, stubborn. Just like your fool father and crazy uncles," she near-shouts. "Okay. That's it," she says menacingly, "I am sitting down and reading these."

Moving with grace to the little table that Bernice used to eat at, she lights a smoke and waits.

Opens the package and organizes the papers into piles.

And waits.

Restless and not quite ready to fulfill the terms of her threat, she strips the bed, puts the soiled bedclothes in the hamper and re-makes the bed with the new linens that the old bird had brought up yesterday. Freda had come up, noted her auntie's agitation and gone back down to the bakery to see if Lola needed any help.

A few minutes later, Auntie Val had been surprised to hear Lola on the stairs and was more shocked by the care package she held in her skinny arms. Candles and incense, cheesecake remainders and sandwiches. Table lamp and magazines, a small cassette player and some tape with what sounded like whales humping or something.

"How's it goin'?" Lola had said in her gruff style, not peeking around or snooping or anything.

"Good, I guess," Valene had hedged. Was Bernice paid up on her rent? she wondered.

"She up an' about yet?" Demanding and something else. Val couldn't put her finger on it, but when she thought about it later she thought the little woman had sounded scared.

"Hmmm. Not yet. I suppose she will get hungry sometime." Auntie Val wasn't sure this was true. It had been a full two weeks since she had gotten there, four since Freda showed up, and no one had actually seen Bernice eat in that time. Still, Val got the sense that The Kid was being fed.

"Well, she loves those radish sandwiches, never seen her pass one up yet. Maybe you could run that under her cake-hole a few times." Lola had laughed and then coughed a deep smoker's cough.

"Uh, does she owe you for . . . ?" Val began.

"Maybe you get tired of sittin' up here. Say, you any good at poker?" she had asked.

"Not any good, but I hold my own," said Auntie Val, an exceptional poker player with a good poker face and the good sense to cover her bets. Growing up in her home, she has no tells. You couldn't have them.

Lola thought about it for a few seconds. "Maybe you could join us next week, that is if you . . ."

"Sure. I'm in."

With that, the inverted mirror images had watched each other slyly as they both turned around.

Auntie Val is listening to that same whale music when she thinks she hears Bernice getting out of the tub. Cocking her ear, she yells, "You're gonna freeze in there, my girl, come out and talk to your auntie."

Still nothing.

She keeps reading the hospital file. Tries her hardest not to think of whales humping.

June 26, 2XXX
Partial thickness burns on hands and feet healing and

Tracey Lindberg

scarring. No infection noted. Colour is mottled on feet, dull
white areas noted on heels and toes.

Vital signs monitored, IV required for fluid loss. Mor-
phine 10 mg subcutaneously. Pt. seems agitated, Ativan 2
mg sublingually administered, IV loxapine 5 mg.

Pt. delirious and muttering.

"Stay away."

"Sorry."

"Tree killer."

❧

Valene Calliou considers herself the next in a long line of
argumentative Cree women. Her *Kohkom* Rose's people were
from Kelly Lake – Kelly Lake where the women hid the men
and children when the Treaty Commissioner came through
looking for a few more Indians to sign their rights away. That
proved to be prescient and the cause of much modern-day dis-
tress. On the one hand, her people (and she does not identify
with her dad's family and never will) have not been colonized
or "Indian Acted" to death. On the other hand, the Callious
and nine other families have no reserve, no treaty rights, no
health care. No money. She is third-generation poor. Doesn't
much matter that her family is not part of the Indian Act.
Except on cheque days and when we need a dentist or glasses, she
often laughs to herself.

She was raised by *Kohkom* Rose. Rose lived in the bush,
still in Kelly Lake territory (although it looked like an oil
company's territory the last time she was there), until she

passed. One hundred and thirteen years old and still smoking. Because she was raised by her *kohkom*, Valene felt obliged to stay with her as she grew less and less able to take care of herself. If she was honest about that time, and she can't be yet, she would admit she needed that time more than the old woman did. The hard time.

One of several hard times.

She tries not to think of that when she is sitting and watching her niece . . . wasting. Val herself had taken to bed at times, but she did that out of avoidance, not what feels to her like cocooning or preparing for a storm. For if Valene were capable of self-reflection, she would note from the healing skin on Bernice's heels, from the cut marks on her arms – starting just above the too-prominent scarring – she would know that Bernice is the next in a long line of women who not only like to argue, but who would not die. Val would see this because Val *is* this. She sighs heavily, looking at the mess that is Bernice, and realizes with a bit of a start that the girl actually looks better than she has seen her looking in years.

"What adventures have you been having, my girl?" she asks Bernice absent-mindedly. Because she most certainly does not want to know.

Valene starts to rub her own scar, absent-mindedly. Under her shirt and across her generous belly.

❧

She was an old spirit, *Kohkom* told her. She had suffered much and would likely have a hard love. She would love hard and she would fight hard, Rose had told her. Her fights were plentiful. When she was young, jealousy lived in her like bacteria, flaring up when it wanted and showing up when unwanted. She did a lot of fighting back then. Always the girls. The girls that flocked around whatever man she had fallen for; and she had only fallen for men who wanted girls to flock.

"*Mah*, why you with that guy?" *Kohkom* had asked her more than twice.

The answer was always quite the same: she wanted to be loved, didn't want to be alone, and wanted to be able to shower someone with affection.

Val was a good lover. She could love someone like no one she had ever met. She loved through booze, infidelity and beatings. She loved poor men, rich men, ugly men and good-looking men. Yep, she figgered she could love just about anyone. Unless. They loved her good. While she loved every one of them, she harboured no love in her heart for any of them. They were just faded pieces of a mélange of men that came and went.

Being a modern bush woman raised by a transforming old woman was rich ground for Val (she had once called the old lady a feminist and she had stomped her toe and yelled, presuming her granddaughter was as deaf as her, "I don't even know what that is – if you ever say it again, I will put you out on your ear"). While she had never heard the word, she was stronger than anyone Valene had ever met, and that includes the eight husbands she had (three of them at one time, was Val's understanding). No one would have dared to hit *Kohkom*. She was like sinew. And, she could kick anyone's ass who crossed her – and some who didn't.

Val had always admired that, and had often wished that she had that in her as well. Val was made of softer stuff, though. If there was a wounded dog on the road, she would pick it up and take it home. If there was a spider in the lodge, she would lift it out. If there was a damaged man in the room, she would pick him up, lift him up and watch as he walked away, healthier and better for her loving. So often had she done this, for so many men, that someone had compared her to the Red Cross: she comes in during an emergency and in the best-case scenario was forgotten about as the traumatized moved on.

Maggie had that gene, too. *Except she stopped caring. Stopped feeling completely.* She swipes her hand across her forehead, willing the memory to go away, worries that Birdie has heard her. Seeing no sign of life, she continues her handiwork, a beautiful beaded shawl. Each stitch taking her elsewhere.

When Maggie left, left everyone behind her (or in front of her, depends how you look at it), Valene had tried to respect her sister's decision. She told people her sister was going to look for Birdie – Val reminds herself never to mention that – but Val knew better. When Maggie was done, and she was so completely finished by the time she gave The Kid to Val, she was through. There was no light left in her when she left, and Valene had always wondered how long ago it went out, how long ago Maggie had checked out.

They had shared a boyfriend, years ago. She was sixteen and her sister was seventeen. Maggie had not known, or so Val chose to believe, but Bernice's louse of a father had been bedding them at the same time. Maggie got pregnant. She often said the better sister won, but that man had begged her to take him with her, anywhere. Away from the responsibility of being a dad, Val wanted to believe. The truth was actually more awful. He had loved her. She had loved him. Maggie had seen it, she was sure of it.

But Val had a secret, too. She did have love in her heart for that louse. She was able to have a child. She had one child. And. Had given her up for adoption after twenty hours of labour in a grimy little health care unit in Beaverlodge. She told only Maggie and knows that secret is safe now. She thinks about that baby as she looks at Birdie lying in the bed before her. She was born two months before Bernice. Perfect. No blotchy birthmark on her forehead and thigh. No red skin, always inflamed, from birth. She was beautiful. Valene used to imagine that she would see her on the street. They would know each other. Embrace. Cry. Forgive. Be a family.

As time went by and she had to see Bernice's dad at every wake, funeral, wedding and birthday, saw him go from sad drunk to mean drunk, she learned to forget her baby. Her girl. Donna Rose, she had wanted to call her. Social Services wouldn't tell her who the parents were or what they had named Val's daughter. She liked to pretend that Bernice's dad (even after all these years, she cannot bring herself to think or say his name) was not the father, that some divine immaculate miracle had taken place in Lac Ste. Anne (she went on the pilgrimage for years and had no difficulty reconciling her trek with a spiritual life lived in the lodge) and she had become pregnant with the love of the spirit. Not "de baby Jesus," as *Kohkom* Rose called him, waving her hand at an entity she did not quite know or believe. Realistically, part of her has always known that she was in no state to raise a child and that some-one with her past with men should never have that responsi-bility. But, still. She wondered.

Wondered what would have happened if her sister's husband had followed her, instead of Maggie. Wondered what would have happened if she and Maggie had not seen Bernice's father at the same moment, him at his best, jigging to beat the band to Drops of Brandy. If Bernice, and not Donna Rose, had been hers. If she had seen her – birthmarks, and ruddied – would she have picked her up, lifted her up and taken her?

"*Mah!*" she cries out, too loud, as she drops a stitch, leav-ing a single red bead dangling.

SKINNY FREDA

Get outta my ass, old woman! Freda thinks, with not one regret at the meanness. The old bird has been hovering close to her since she got to the house. Freda will be the first to admit that she likes the attention, but Lola's attention today seems cloying. And her perfume! Eau de toe, Freda smiles to herself.

"Somethin' on your mind, hon?" Lola asks over quite possi-bly the longest cigarette ash that Freda has ever seen.

"Just thinking," Freda says, her mind snapping to attention.

"Worried about your cousin?" Lola clucks sympathetically.

Freda recognizes a little grain of something in her and she bridles with annoyance. It's not jealousy, but Lola's mothering is getting under her skin.

"I 'spose so," Skinny Freda allows.

"Don't worry, The Kid is made of strong stuff, she is gonna be just fine," Lola hopes out loud.

Freda sees it again, a flicker of something so, so hungry? on Lola's face that she is immediately annoyed. She knows she shouldn't be. Somehow the old woman had figured out how to find her, and then when Freda called her Auntie Val, Lola had picked her up at the bus depot in her old Malibu when she showed up. They had been camping above and in the bakery ever since.

Freda worries that Lola's ash will drop into the batch of dough they are making for cinnamon buns.

Lola is one of those people who makes smoking look terrible, Freda thinks. Her skin is too taut and leathery and the lines in her mouth are deeply entrenched on what Freda thinks is a surprisingly pretty face. They stare at each other for a moment and both look away and at their own hands as they pound the dough.

Freda's hands are remarkably soft. Deep brown with little age showing on them, they are quite nimble and strong. Her fingers ply the concoction and she frowns with concentration, willing Lola to stop fortheloveofgod talking. She reaches up with a clean finger and flicks on the radio. The music is warm and drum heavy and the sound fills the little kitchen. It sounds like an Honour Song, but she is not familiar with it. She stops cold when she hears Lola singing the song an octave higher and trilling in between the beat.

How the fuck . . . Freda thinks. Shocked.

Lola, for her part, just keeps on pounding the doughy batter, now to the rhythm of the drum song.

There is no way, no earthly way that this old *moniaskwew* has ever heard the song before. Yet, there she stands pounding and singing like she is at an intertribal. Freda can't quite get her head around this and quietly resumes her work, listening for some indication that Lola is just making it up as she goes along. Lola, in a rare moment of self-awareness, can feel the quiet in the room. She looks up but sees her work partner is focused on the task at hand and begins to blush furiously.

Freda is not stunned that Lola knows a pow wow song *by heart*. She is shocked that Lola doesn't know that she knows it. For, if you were to ask Freda she would tell you that *moniaw* always want you to know what they think they know. And. She should know. She has dated them almost exclusively.

The first white boy she dated was in high school. Phil Filmore. She looked him up on the Facebook last year and saw a doughy bald man who she would not have known. He was, in her experience, like most *moniawak* who dated Indian women: outsider, fringe dweller, attracted to the otherness but insisting it was sameness that attracted them. What he also was, was exceedingly gentle. He was passive to a degree that still sits with Freda. Only showing affection if prodded, making a move only if she ignored him, he was easy to read and to like. So, while she supposed he liked her best when she did not like him (he only ever asked her out when she had a boyfriend), she enjoyed the easy pattern of his lust and his smart conversation.

What Freda learned from him, and what she still lives by today, is that men are simple. And that *moniaw* men who are drawn to Indian women are men who live on the outside of white society. She imagines that gentle Phil is now trying to bed all of his now-married ex-girlfriends in order to keep being unwanted, and that he enjoys the elementary nature of relationships without strings more than the reminiscence of the relationships they had. Since then, there has been a long list of *moniawak* – not too long. Freda looks for men when she wants company and keeps them around if they are good company. She has always been one of those women who has a boyfriend, but you can never quite remember his name. She is also one of those women who is allied with strong women, so she will be the first to check out of a relationship if there is something better to do with her friends. Or family.

She has a little shudder of guilt, thinking of her cousin up in bed above them. Birdie had looked so grey when she got there. And her eyes. Her eyes looked like she had left already or was well on her way. Lately, Freda has given herself peace by thinking that Birdie is fasting. Sure, it's been more than four days, but some journeys and cleansings take longer.

Back before Maggie left, and way before Bernice went to the San, Freda and Bernice used to see each other every other weekend when some uncle or other would take Freda to the city to visit. *That shithole of an apartment,* she recalls. How long has Valene lived there? she wonders. Fifteen years? It wasn't the filth of Pecker Palace that got to her – it was the desperation caulked in the cracks. Stumbling drunks, muttering madmen and soiled women walked around, and around (never in, but clearly they lived there), the apartment block. Freda could smell the gave-up coming through their skin; feel the sadness radiating off their backs. Still, she resented that Birdie got to live with Auntie Val (fun Val! before they found out she was Loony Val!), go to a special girls' school and eat at an A&W once in a while. When she went to visit her there the first time, when she was going to that nuns' school, Bernice would barely talk, settled in to the CBC and watching that fat bastard chef while Freda went crazy trying to get her to walk with her to the mall.

"Berniiiiiiice, I will write down the recipes, let's just get out of here for a while!" she would wheedle.

And Bernice, who hid herself in her room until the uncle left, and hid herself behind the TV screen while her cousin waited for her, would stare at her blankly for a second before returning to her show.

"You don't even cook the stuff, for fuck's sake," Freda had pushed out between gritted teeth. Once.

Bernice looked at her, surprised, and said, "But I am going to." Freda was so angry that she grabbed her purse (which had leather tassels on it), stomped out so that her boots struck the floor (with more leather tassels vibrating) and headed to the mall on her own. There she met some Phil or other and had giggly phone calls (him) that carried on until her next visit. Then there was another Phil and another.

Her most recent Phil was two weeks before she came to Gibsons. He was only part Phil, because he was Metis. She wasn't sure about that, though, because he pronounced it "Met-tiss." He was gentle. He was sweetly dull. And. He never laid a hand on her. When she got Lola's call ("You Bernice's cousin or something?"), she had dropped Phil, hopped a series of hitches and got to her cousin's side within twenty-four hours. And. Oh God. She looked and smelled terrible. When

Tracey Lindberg

she hunted around her little apartment, she found that fucking CBC poster of that stupid Pat John and the same Aer Lingus bag that Bernice had been carrying since she was ten. And. The file. She knew what was in that file and didn't want to know what was in it. So, it wasn't so much honouring Bernice or respecting her privacy as letting the dead stay dead.

If that fucker kills her, I will go dig him up and grind his bones, she had thought.

For Bernice appears to be truly dying. She had shorn her hair off (did she know about Maggie?), has lost a lot of weight, and clearly has given up on any notion of personal hygiene. If she had had a Phil with her, Freda would have insisted on throwing Bernice in a tub, but she found (as she often found in these instances) that Phils just couldn't get it. She didn't want to explain a fast, a vision, a change, or even the fucking tightwad chef. She didn't want to explain Bernice's "absence," the San or that night. She just wanted her cousin, her opposite-in-every-way cousin, to come back.

And. Truth be told, Skinny Freda is pissed off. That she is pissed off indicates one of two things: someone has fucked with her, or she is scared. And while Bernice might be fucking with her, Freda tastes something in the back of her throat while she looks at her cousinsister: an overwhelming need to protect.

It is likely ironic that she wants to take care of her big cousin now, after Bernice had quite possibly severed the only tie that genetically bound them. She might not know the word, but she knows the actuality: irony. After years of quietly feeling superior to Bernice because of her cousin's weight and appearance, she finds something else in her throat when she sees Bernice in bed at Lola's: a wellspring of unshed tears. She is confounded to find, as she stares at Bernice's soiled and oily form, that they are not tears of sadness but of something else: she is a bit proud of her cousin. Again, she doesn't know the words, but it's something like her commitment to silence and solitude. Freda knows she could never do that. This.

And while she resents what she thinks Bernice got – to live in Edmonton with her auntie, taken into care by that white couple and even living on the streets in Edmonton before . . . before that day and the San – she knows inside of her that Bernice may be, for the first time, making a choice.

She chose differently. Like Birdie, she had her secrets. It was just easier to hide when you were not so big. Freda did not hide in Phils. Phils hid in her. She found herself too visible in silence; exposed in the quiet of reflection. So, Freda had made the decision never to be quiet. Sit quiet. Think in solitude. For a time, when she was ten or so and back when she left Maggie's, she hid with booze. It quieted down the noise inside and amplified the sound outside. Each sip snuck. Each slug stolen. Each gulp of glasses forgotten. A return to welcome noise. Living on her own, even for that brief time when she lived with her auntie in town (all the troublegirls got sent to Auntie Val) when things were particularly bad, it was easy to be noisy. There was a constant stream of people, strays, wandering in and out. Each wanting the space filled with sound.

When Valene moved to Edmonton, Freda slept almost any-where. Almost. She would stay with people, homes with strong matriarchs, until the noise inside came back or someone's old man looked at her too long, or the wisp of annoyance followed her into a room. Dirty old men. She was twelve. Once when those things happened, she just left. No one to account to, no place to be. No one to belong to. No family.

If Birdie left her . . .

A bang! in her imagination shakes the memories loose and for a while Freda sits in the chair at the table, watching Bernice over the top of a *National Enquirer*. If Bernice had tried to read Skinny Freda's face, she would have seen that there is nothing there. A little wariness is all that her muscles betray. Too tired to ask, and because she only has pissed off or scared to resort to, Freda chooses anger. And. She is definitely not talking to Bernice yet. Something draws her attention to her no–longer–so-fat cousin. Something is missing. Or. There is something new there. She can't put her finger on it, but Bernice somehow looks less Here.

After a while, Freda grows tired of staring at Bernice and begins to play solitaire. The snap snap snaps of her long nails, flipping the cards into order.

acimowin

And when she got to that little tree
She saw that
it was dying.
No one looked after it
And it was curling up.
There was a fire coming
Her birdself knew it but
couldn't do anything.
All the other animals came and sat by it
but they couldn't do anything.
So she started walking
until it got too hot.
Then she flew.
High.
And so high
She didn't hear a sound.

Tracey Lindberg

8

WHERE SHE WAS

kakosoweht: s/he is the one who is afraid of people

pawatamowin

She dreams she has one song, one mournful song. Soars at night and stays quiet in the day. She wakes one night. To bars. And knows in her sleepless sleep that she is caged.

I N CARE, ONCE SOCIAL SERVICES TOOK HER FROM VAL, Bernice made herself as small as possible, as unnoticeable as could be, but still they found her.

"Hey, fat bitch, get outta my way."

"You fat cow, you're in my chair."

"Yo! Buffalo – move it."

It seemed that no matter where she was, where she went, she was in the way. Even curled in her little cot, taking as little space as possible (reading, not looking up, not listening for anything but someone approaching her), she seemed to be the epicentre of some unkindness. Some of the other residents were fine, but on the whole she was ignored. There was a toughness pecking order that left her close enough to crazy to be left largely alone. Even so, Bernice knew that to speak was to be noticed, and she did not want that.

It came as a relief when a British family took her into their home as a foster child. The Ingelsons, with no children of their own, picked her up a few weeks before her sixteenth birthday. It was easy to be quiet with the Ingelsons as they were forever talking.

"I don't know, Bernice, I like the pink one better, but it's your prom." Ann said sweetly (and Ann said everything sweetly), "Which one do you like?"

Bernice definitely liked the pink one, it was a light and frilly dress with layers of soft fabric in different shades of pink frothing together in a confection that was age, gender and occasion appropriate. Of course Ann was right, Ann was always right. That's why she was awarded "Foster Parent of the Year" three years ago. And that was exactly why Bernice was leaning towards the turquoise dress.

"I don't care, whatever," Bernice said, definitely caring and not at all willing to accept whatever.

Ann was perplexed. Bernice had been hemming and hawing all day, this was supposed to be a lot more fun than it had been and her patience was, she was sure, being tested.

"Well," she thought out loud, doing the calculations, "we could take them both home and you could decide later? Then, we could bring one back . . . or keep it if you want."

Bernice headed back to the change room and closed the door so Ann wouldn't hear her crying. She had wanted a fight, words of some sort, and this was somehow worse. As she wishes, whatever she wants, she should choose. She buckled under the weight of this degree of autonomy and felt the walls of the change room begin to push at her.

"Bernice? Maybe we could just keep both, and then you could have a dress just in case . . ." Ann feels bad, she knows, and this made Bernice cry harder. Soundless crying in change room three of Fanny's Finery. What did she have to be sorry about, anyhow? More importantly, what were these "just in cases" that kept coming up? Just in case she decided to dress inappropriately and head to the reserve? Just in case she wanted to rub everyone's nose in her good fortune? Just in case Bernice had a hearing and she really wanted to deck herself out for it?

With thoughts of returning, she steeled herself. In her head, she saw moving into Ann and Tom's place as a choice that no one made for her. She couldn't stay at Ann and Tom's forever, she knew that, but she would have liked to pretend that she was so she didn't feel so bad all of the time.

"Bernice? Birdie, are you all right?" Ann asked her tenderly.

The tenderness also hardened her resolve. If, when, she left these people she would have to do it like the provincial park signs say: "Please leave nothing but footprints, please take nothing but pictures." She didn't want them to hurt and worry when she goes, because she definitely had to go. Definitely, but after the prom, she supposed.

"I'm okay, just a little tired. Let's get the pink one, okay?" One pink dress could not hurt.

One canopy bed, one fish tank, one set of back-to-school clothes, one trip home every couple of weeks, one amazing sleepover birthday party with no locks on the door, one trip to Vancouver Island, one computer, one bookcase and all the books she needs, one package of envelopes with stamps on them, her own bathroom and three good meals a day were not too much, were they?

The first two months she was at their house, Ann and Tom didn't ask anything of her. No one ever went in her room and it was her responsibility to keep it clean. It wasn't until the pork incident, as Ann and Tom laughingly called it to dinner guests, that she felt some sort of peace in the house. The peace, she thought, came about when she was no longer waiting for the other shoe to drop.

Every day, Bernice offered to clean the table and set the dishwasher. In this time, she would have forty-five minutes to herself. What no one mentioned in the telling of the story that has become dinner fodder was that she always did the

Tracey Lindberg

dishes. And kept the kitchen and dining room immaculate. This was important to Bernice. Not because it justified her actions, but because it spoke to her good character.

But all that anyone remembered, in the infamous storytelling that she has sat through on three occasions now, was this: Ann caught her storing fresh food under her bed. In her perfect room with the canopy bed.

"And I kind of thought that something wasn't right, that there were kitchen smells where there shouldn't be any," Ann said kindly, looking at Bernice kindly, transmitting her kindness kindly to her kind guests who look at Bernice less kindly, not understanding Ann's kindness but wanting to emulate being kind.

"This sweet little girl was afraid," hushed and conveying shock, "that we would run out of food!" The horror of the notion and of Bernice's supposed past fills the dining room. Takes the place of the food that was hidden under the bed.

They could take a flying leap as far as Bernice was concerned. She wasn't afraid that they would run out of food, she needed food should she decide to run. There was always food to be had at home. Sure, sometimes you had to plan more and work harder for it, but there was always an aunt or uncle, or *Kohkom*, to turn to in a pinch. And, yes, most certainly, the Meetooses had more pinches than the Ingelsons. But that was the result of history and design, not some flaw in her family or her people. When she leaves the Ingelsons' and is street living in Edmonton – learning about protection, pride, loyalty, danger and madness – THAT will feel less like a pinch than living with the white couple.

Somehow, amazingly, when Bernice brought her report card home all was forgiven. Those *A*s on the paper convinced the Ingelsons that everything was all right with Bernice. That they were doing something or everything right. And because the delivery of the report card coincided with a late-night confession Bernice made to her caregivers about the origin of her chosen name, Ann and Tom began to call her Birdie. She associated it with their assessment of her goodness. If she was good, she was Birdie. She didn't mind it at first. It allowed her to try on a persona — one which was able to try happiness, could feel happiness. When she was free and happy, she called herself Birdie, just as her family had. Like Maggie had when she allowed herself tenderness. If she made inconsistent statements or seemed reticent, she was Bernice. She tried not to feel disloyal and tried doubly hard not to resent them for calling her Birdie when she had not earned it. In truth, she often had to work at not begrudging them, resenting them. But was it her fault they couldn't have children? Could she be blamed for wanting their acreage (on "ancient Indian land" as Tom intones after two Scotches), their refrigerator that makes ice and their complete lack of guilt over their fortune? Years later, at the San, she will remember the luxury of being absolutely provided for when her meals are made, schedules are written and activities are provided. At the Ingelsons' though, she felt resentment more than peace with the provisioning.

Sometimes she felt shame at her mean thoughts. When she thought of all that the women in her family have done to make sure that she gets anywhere safe. And the Ingelsons tried, after all. They were particularly sweet to her, putting a lock on her door, letting her call home whenever she wanted, and driving her to Little Loon on the rare occasions she asked to go.

"Be good," Auntie Val told her every time she walked out the door, back to the new Jeep Cherokee. No one told her to think good. To feel good. As if she knew what that meant, anyhow.

Back then, she would later realize, she didn't understand that kindness was unconditional. In truth, the Ingelsons were profoundly sweet, if unwitting, accessories to her escape from family. From the uncles. They were just a place for her to stop, breathe and get her bearings before she made a break for it.

Ann and Tom treated her warmly, like (the strange cousin at the reunion to whom no one talks) family. She had moments of real tranquility, pieces of peace, that she will hold close to her like a jewel. Never comfortable around men, she and Tom signed a gentle truce. She sat with him in the living room and talked, every night, with Ann in the kitchen or at the dining room table. If Ann left those rooms, Bernice would go to hers. No one ever mentioned it and it did not seem odd, even as she became an adult, not to spend time alone with a man.

She and Ann would sit together for hours, sewing, canning, baking or knitting. It was understood that their hands would always be moving; it was like their hands were the motors that generated their mouths. They came to appreciate a companionable silence, too, and it was in their home that Bernice learned that silence could be empty like a bubble and that quiet was not fuelled by tension. No one ever spoke of what had happened, what her past was like. Neither of the Ingelsons seemed to worry about when she would leave. While she was still a teenager (although not for long), though, Ann did make mention of a store in town that wanted a clerk. Bernice tried not to knead the bread she was working with any more energy than usual. Attempted to regularize her breathing. Channelled only good thoughts to her food. Once she was done, and the loaves were in the oven, she went to her room and took an inventory of what she would take with her when she left: poster tube, Aer Lingus bag and one suitcase filled with paper, clothes and books. She was not so dramatic as to leave a note when she left a few weeks later. However, in the flour on the cupboard that she did not wash before she set buns aside to rise (and which Ann would be able to bake when she got home) she spelled out "Family."

In the years that passed, she thought of that sometimes as she sat alone and read. She wishes she could tell kid Bernice that the years she spends with the Ingelsons will be the best of her life. She is in no shape to give anyone advice. If she did have the wherewithal to advise anyone, she would have told them: It is easier to be big than little. Say what you want, but the flesh jacket did its job. She found that she could hide in a crowd and walk late at night. She ran from the Ingelsons to the only other nowhere she knew (Edmontonians might be angry to know it was a netherworld for some). It was different that time. She barely recognizes the place where she lived with her auntie when she went to the Academy years before. She was changed, too. She was eighteen and out of the grasp of uncles. But eighteen meant something else to a whole other group of men, especially if you lived on the streets.

She felt, at times, invisible. That helped. She could change, too. She could appear and disappear, using only words to

Tracey Lindberg

unmask herself. Some people, mostly crazy people, could see her. Not that anyone recognized her. She wore black only, hid in crowds and walked the city streets with her eyes down. Some days, on the best of days, she met women's eyes – only street women – women who were the seen/unseen. On other days, she felt oddly disconnected from her body, like she did not know the nature of her form.

She spent her days walking, endless walking, and would go for weeks without saying a word to anyone. Smiling like she had a secret, she planned her days around getting someplace to sleep by nine at night. This had proven incredibly easy and impossible, depending on the day, the pay period, the weather and her ability to be seen. Every so often, when she saw someone from home, she tried immediately to become invisible. One night she was sure she saw a cousin near her former residence. Pecker Palace. A former home. It almost made her smile. That time, as it did most often, it worked.

When she was needful, when it felt safer than not, and when she understood the need around her as hungry but not desperate, she would let herself be seen by men. Or a man. Always alone. Always someplace where she knew the safety exits. Then, she shifted her shape and became a woman whom other people admired but still feared. It was easier to be big than little, especially then.

Some days, when she was still and when she had will, she could absolutely disappear. From herself as well as others. She knew she could separate who she was from where she was; that shift had started years before. But, at a certain point that separation changed not only people's ability to see her, but her ability to see herself. She began to lose time. It was actually more of an intentional shifting of gears in time. By the time she got to the San, she had perfected it. In Edmonton, though, it was still an imprecise, unmapped trip. Where she went depended upon something that she could not control. All she knew was that she usually ended up someplace where the past lives with the present, and they mingled like smoke. Once it cleared, she was almost sure she would see her future. She never did, though.

As she began to really understand the nature of her inheritance – when time welcomed her in and sent her back – Bernice was mostly unafraid of the forgotten travel. When she came back, she would come back to treasures. She was rarely surprised and often delighted at her bounty. Edible gifts in her pockets or in her Safeway cart (she imagines, to those people who can see her, that she looks like a shopping cart lady; she realizes with a start that she actually is one and laughs, a big belly and full of delight laugh). Few would understand the joy of looking into a bag and finding a delicately braided length of dried sweetgrass. A tin filled with dried herbs that she did not recognize. Gingerly, like she was burying something precious, she would cover them and put them in the bottom of her cart. Other times, she would find herself weeding through garbage like it was a treasure chest. Old socks and a torn Gap T-shirt got stuffed into her cart amongst tin boxes, a bulletin board and a hot water bottle. She had imagined herself a raccoon, small and fragile hands moving quickly over the bounty, starting at the sound of others approaching. She would smile and stand straight when she found something that made her richer. It was like an endless hunt, except she had no map, no clues and there was no discernible treasure. Just scraps in a shopping cart, things a crow might collect, nothing so heavy that she couldn't grab it quickly and run. And, if it seemed endless, the time ran together and rushed by her like droplets in a springtime stream. Her years in the city (which had a forest in it, deer through it and the odd moose lost within it) were divided into two times of day: dangerous time and safe time. For her, nighttime mostly was safer. She could hide in the corner tables of darkened bars – being the only sober one made her automatically more aware of any danger. She could hide in the hotel rooms of people who were flush and wait until they passed out to dig out her treasures or surf the ancient TVs for cooking shows or reruns of *The Beachcombers*. When she could not find a place to sleep by nine, she wandered. Nighttime sometimes allowed her to find quiet in crowds and luxury in squalor. The day times were scarier. She was, just by her sheer size, recognizable. There was no hiding in the rushing downtown traffic. No rushing away from the too-large spotlight of the gleam of morning light. No avoiding contact in spaces where people brushed up against strangers and shared space with enemies. There was no way to hide your treasure in a spotlight, no time to grab your belongings when people could approximate your capacity to get away.

Yes, in the city four years could pass by you like the rock in that stream because the alleys and skyscrapers are largely unchanged with the seasons. Weather does not impact your hunt, only how cold your sleep will be.

It was harder to dream in the city. When she first got there and after she would not allow grief to be her travelling companion, she pretended that the white noise of traffic was the sound of crisp snow pelting the aluminum siding of a trailer. It allowed her to sleep better, being soothed by the parallel urban life. For a while, she pretended that the poorly loaded trucks bouncing down potholed streets were cracks of thunder and that the thunder spirits were closer and unsettled on the city skyscape. After the first year, the squealing of old brake pads no longer sounded like the keening nasally caw of ducks. It became what it was, white noise in the white city. After a few months of going to visit her every so often, she looked for and avoided her Auntie Val, by turns. Part of her was so hurt at being taken from the Pecker Palace, part of her was guilty for getting a good life with the Ingelsons. She could avoid family, but it would always find her.

Once in a while, she would run into (not be able to run from) relatives in the mall downtown or on the street.

"Where you been, cousin?" some asked, knowing precisely where she had not been: home. She had built up a thick veneer of unknowingness, a fully constructed naïveté that Cree politeness would allow to stand in the face of impolite questions.

"Heard you had a white family now," one not-so-polite relative asked/told her.

"Seen your mom lately?" another said pointedly.

She would nod or not nod and be sure not to ask about anything other than immediate concerns. Accidents and wonder were something she didn't believe in, then. She wasn't so sure about family, either.

One time, when Bernice was very small, she imagined she was lost in the bush. She was not – no one would have allowed that – but she had convinced herself she was miles from the other women. It was just spring, some ice still clung to the branches of the low-lying trees, and she sat amongst the branches of a pine tree until she was far away from her tiny room under the stairs, miles away from her uncle Larry's pickup truck and hours from the reserve. She'd thought herself hopelessly and happily lost until Skinny Freda had said, "C'monnnnn, Bernice, you're slowing us down."

Even then, she had hidden in quiet. No one spoke to her on the way home and no one noticed when she slipped away to the cubbyhole under the stairs.

As she entered her teens and really started to gain weight, her room felt less like a cupboard-turned-bedroom and more like a jacket that she slipped into when she needed warmth. She believed that if she got big enough there would be no room in there for anyone but her.

In her current darkness at Lola's, she wills her hand to reach for the string attached to the stairs in her childhood room which she pulled to turn on the light. In the outer world, her gesture is a twitch in her right hand. She can't reach the string.

The sounds of the house late at night come to her, and she hears pots in the bakery kitchen, Freda setting the table and the muffled sound of CBC North on the radio. These sounds are safe.

But Bernice is no longer there.

She was sitting in the truck with all of her uncles. The Ingelsons had dropped her off for a visit. Wishing she had stayed in her mom's empty house, instead she was silent and quieted and filled with ill. A cramped Chevy truck, pockets full of cash and a dashboard filled with cigarettes and junk food. Headed to the city for groceries. When everyone decided to spend a portion of the money on booze, Bernice steadfastly refused to leave the truck or let go of the cheque until, angrily, they all went to the Safeway and spent the money as originally planned.

"You're fucking crazy," her uncle Larry had spat at her. Freda sat in the back, seemingly oblivious, but willing them not to see or think about her. If Birdie pulled her in, which she never did, she would be visible, on the uncles' radar. Open for the season. But Birdie never did, and resolutely she stared straight ahead as the uncles circled.

"She's not even here," griped the second-least-kind uncle. "She's off in that fucking dream world so she doesn't have to . . ."

"Shhhh," warned a kinder uncle. "We all got that same world to go to. Maybe you should go there, too."

They turn up the radio.

Hey-ya-hey ay yay yah hah.
Hey-ya-hey-ay-yay-yah-hah.
Hey ay yay hey yah
Hey ay yay hah.

Tracey Lindberg

Her Gibsons self stiffens at the recall. Her spirit wanders.

She was under the stairs. In her room. Soft tiptoes and breath held tightly in his chest like a secret, coming down the stairs and listening. Paused and listened. For her. For her breathing. For her fear, she imagined. Soft shuffling past her door. And back again. Waiting for the awake sounds of others. She held her breath and pressed her legs against the door – she did this while lying sideways across her bed.

The inevitable shaky hand on the latch. Husky breathing. Scared? No. Something different. She didn't know this breath. Pushing on the door. Firmly. Sure. And. Then. Angrily. With force. And might. Pushing her girl legs back until they buckle at useless girl knees. The lighter black of the hallway replacing the pitch of her cubby. And. Then black again.

In Gibsons, Bernice lies still as a thistle on a hot summer's day.

Hey-ya–hey ay yay yah hah.
Hey-ya–hey-ay-yay-yah-hah.
Hey ay yay hey yah
Hey ay yay hah.

If Bernice notices the drumbeat intensifying and pounding with more vigour, she gives no sign. Her skin feels a tingle, a notice of change, and if she were awake she would expect to find herself changed back to her regular form, in her regular body and in a place she hadn't known she had gone to. The shift, she would have imagined, made her stronger and more resilient.

What she could not know is that it has also made her cognizant of time as an arch and not a line. In the shift she had been preparing for her whole life, Bernice who is not Bernice is able to move back and forth like a laser on a CD changer. She does not have the cognizance of her body and surroundings as she did in life. She has, instead, the distinct impression of a being disconnected from the living but even more intricately connected to life. The body is not hers. She is annoyed. Freda is mooning around her like she has lost her best friend. With dismay, Bernice notices that the formerly fat body she had (she wondered if, like Prince, she could get a symbol for that) is soiled. She wants to tell Freda, anyone, to clean that up. It is humiliating enough to be half dead with an almost boob hanging out. But this? Too much. No one should have to see their body failing them. *Earth body failing earth me*, she thinks.

In a way, she supposes that this is for the best – sometime she is going to have to talk to her and Lola. Not to mention Auntie Val. She is not ready yet, though. She has "some business to attend to," as *Kohkom* Maria would say heading out the door to church. Serious business, as the song says. Only with a stronger drumbeat.

She sees herself. In the continuum of time that has graced her. From her bird's-eye view she sees. Then. Not. Now. Sees who her bodily self became: huge, bigger than she knew, and her shoulders, stooped like she had lost something. A fight. A friend. A life. She was wearing the yellowed top and bottoms from the San, a male patient's outfit.

That big body of the girl she occupied sat hunched over

a desk, writing in a journal. That girl had bandages on her hands and was writing fitfully.

That girl was not honest in that – she didn't think she could be at the time. If she had the energy to write it all down now she would have more stuff to say. About things. But really, who knew any sort of truth at twenty-one? At twenty-four? Would she really have been able to be honest, at that? Although, really, it was the THAT she did not want to talk about. But it was in her head and she didn't want it to stay there. She wrote out a timeline. Didn't know eventually that she would forget time entirely and fly back and forth between places. Here. There. And time. Now. Then.

Little things keep bubbling over into her changeworld. Like that crazy Freda, who says to that body over 'n over again, "It's not your fault." Isn't that crazy? Even in her non-Bernice form, the one which had tuned her cousin out for years, she could still be gotten to by that Skinny Freda. She imagines that Freda has something spilling out of her like water from a boiling kettle. Not rage. Guilt or remorse or some ugly cousinemotion. But, like *Moshom* said, "There's no friend like an old friend." Freda is Bernice's oldest friend. She who never sat beside her. Was not there all through her troubles, in courtrooms, in bathrooms, in waiting rooms, hospitals and visitors' rooms. Bernice had forgotten about that when she would allow herself to ragemember. And she could also not forget Freda's shaky lip when the door was kicked closed in front of her. The knowing in her eyes. She knew. At the very least, Freda had noticed. And. Was relieved. That. It was not. Her.

In her mind's eye, Bernice sees Auntie Val. Her memory

loops through time to an afternoon when Bernice and her auntie sang Andy Gibb and danced to ABBA. No one, no one on the rez or in the settlement was singing Andy Gibb and dancing to ABBA. One of those afternoons, Auntie Val had said to Freda that she was Bernice's friend because she was the only one who fit in her room with her. Val didn't know Bernice could hear her, and today, Bernice realizes that her auntie was not being mean. In Cree territory, that would be a compliment, Bernice knows. What she also knows is that her auntie was naming the protection that the girls provided to each other when they stuck together; they could block out the world together. She was insulating Bernice's scared/sacred self with what protection she could find. Now, upon reflection, Bernice supposes that she was right. A little. Her auntie still had a mean mouth when she drank. But from that she knew the truth that no one talked about: Freda belonged to no one. They were friends and not bloodcousins. She was more friend than cousin because she had no bloodtie. She was family because they were sworn to each other through the ugliest of adoption rituals.

Her mind flits back and forth, looking around, like someone trying to pause a DVD. Sees Big Bernice and an even skinnier Skinny Freda in the Little Loon house mooning over *The Beachcombers* on TV. What appears is what Bernice never knew: Freda did not even like Jesse. She just pretended to for Bernice. And, most disturbing, Freda seemed to be a little crazy obsessed with Hughie. Stranger things have happened, Birdie supposes.

She starts to enjoy silence instead of dreading its interruption. When Auntie Val goes to the market, she comes back with game and berries. When Freda goes, she brings seafood and rare and out-of-season herbs and plants. When Lola shops, she gathers cuisine and foods that no one has heard of before. And. The list. None is a particularly inspired cook, but each finds herself trying new recipes and stockpiling ingredients. Left alone when the three women go to cook, Bernice is able to feel exhaustion rumble off of her and into the room.

At each meal, the three women cook beside each other. When they go to the kitchen Bernice seems equally unaware of their presence and of their absence, but if she were to awaken and go downstairs, she would most likely faint in shock to learn that Freda has assumed her portion of the duties in the bakery. Besides the odd lout, Freda never takes anything seriously. Cooking for Bernice and learning from the insolent wheezing chef on the television seem to consume the tiny brown woman.

Each day, Freda puts on baker's whites and soft shoes so that you could barely hear her going down the stairs. It is almost like she had chosen quiet over noisy for once. If Bernice knows, if Bernice is present, she would think that noisy was going to be awful lonely without Freda by its side.

Bernice has been immersed in travelling, lately. The three women moving around her generate some sort of resistance that allows her to travel back and forth (Now and Then, Here and There) without much pain. Somewhere in the back of her mind there is an idea. A memory. A piece of something yet unearthed. Regardless, in some sort of inverted mathematical equation, home no longer lives in her and she can visit it with a tourist's senses. As a result, she travels to/thinks about home every day now. Sometimes, if she listens closely, she can hear the hum of traffic from the provincial highway that cut through the reserve. (How crazy was that – to put a highway right in the middle of the reserve?) If it gets quiet in the bakery she can imagine that she is sitting near the summer kitchen watching *Kohkom* pound dry meat. She hears the thump thump thump of her wooden hammer on the tough give of the moose meat. They used to dip it in butter and eat whole pieces like bread. Even the old ladies would chew it until their mouths glistened and the meat was soft again. *Kohkom* would make enough for everyone, but she always stashed a little away for herself and her favourite granddaughter to take with them on their walks. Sometimes they would take Freda, but she was so noisy that *Kohkom* would tell stories about noisy girls until she was quiet.

Bernice misses her. She only wishes that *Kohkom* had passed on before the trouble started. She wonders if *Kohkom* saw her boys turn into . . . something. She is saddened to find she is relieved that *Kohkom* was gone by the time of the fire. She doesn't know if she could have borne the look in her *kohkom*'s eyes after what happened. She is just starting to piece that stuff together now, and doesn't know that it made sense before this. She misses her every day and will miss her most when she has her ceremony; *Kohkom* taught her how to be a woman.

When she was eleven, Bernice got her first bra. It was a woman's bra – no neat and petite trainer set with a tiny pink rose for her. No, Bernice's bra had six hooks and eyes at the back and thick white straps capable of confining the heartiest of bosoms.

Tracey Lindberg

Kohkom Rose had come to the city, picked her up from the Pecker Palace and taken her shopping for the day, and there was none of the *Seventeen* awkwardness or glee in that trip. There was a certain comfort in having someone so assured make decisions at such an embarrassing time. Still, it was hard to remember that when her *kohkom* whipped out a piece of twine, wrapped it around her rib cage and passed it to the wide-eyed sales clerk.

"*This big*," she had said.

She was this big.

She and *Kohkom* wordlessly shopped as the clerk brought big *kohkom* bras and Bernice, red-faced and breathless, stomped to the change room to try them on. In her shyness, she eventually took the bra that looked the least like bras in the magazines, the only one that fit around her sweater, T-shirt and jacket.

She had that bra for eight years. Eight years. That was longer than she had lived in any place. Longer than *The Beachcombers* was on the air (if you don't count syndication, which she doesn't – because if they don't look like that now it doesn't count). She threw it out on her nineteenth birthday. That year she felt like the bra looked: too small and too big, grey and worn at the edges. She had carried it in her cart for a few weeks until other priorities arose. Underwear was not her worry at the cusp of her twenties. Footwear had taken over.

She feels uncomfortable when Freda changes her clothes for her, but mostly she is ashamed that she has no bras. Eventually, Freda buys her a pretty purple set. ("This oughta cheer ya up. Nothing like something frilly to perk a girl up.") Every day in the beginning of this, this journey from the bed, when that bra was washed and replaced, she had shirked it off and put it under the bed. She noticed her breasts at these times, they are becoming much smaller and flatter and they droop on her now smaller body. She wonders sometimes how much weight she has lost and thinks the bed no longer creaks beneath her when she moves. It could be that she moves less, hears little, but those flattened breasts tell the real story.

When she was getting breasts she could smell the excitement around her. In men, in kitchens, at dances. It was like some strange boob chemical had been released and it didn't allow anyone to look her in the face for more than a minute. She was a favourite at dances because she didn't say anything when boymen surreptitiously rubbed themselves against her. Frozen with panic, she was dragged to and from the dance floor without ever uttering a word.

On a particularly hot night at the community hall she had sat in a bathroom stall for three hours, feet pulled up and sizable buttocks perched on a toilet with no seat. She heard girl-women talk about each other and then hug outside her door. Heard her family maligned and herself denigrated. *Slut, tease, hussy, cow, cunt, bitch, whore, hooker, pro, ass peddler, cooze.*

"She fucks everyone, you know. Has for years."

"I heard she blew Johnny Morrissey last weekend at the hockey game."

"Hope she doesn't fall over tonight, she's carrying a big load."

She hoped she didn't fall over either. One night when she had come to visit from the Ingelsons' – she must have been about sixteen – in a sad state, she drank to deafness and was falling all over the hall when her mother came up, grabbed her arm and threw her into the truck. "Don't you shame us like that ever again, Bernice."

"They're laughin' at us anyhow, nothin' I can do can change that," she sneered. For the first time in her life, her mother smacked her one. "Don't you dare let your uncles' shame come home to you." She stared at her daughter hard.

Shame? She didn't know the half of it, Bernice thinks. She can feel that flush, that horrible red, spread to her pale staring face. Even on this bed, miles and years away, she feels the disgrace of her first realization: that was the first night that she knew that she was not quite right. Sure, she has always been quiet, something of a loner and a little strange by anyone's standards. But that night, deaf and blind, it was all she could do not to faint from the stench of her mother's anger. She knows she could smell pain then, but she isn't sure that she has ever led a life without that gift. She is too aware of the hurt around her. Sympathy pain. When the smell dissipated, she was staring into her mom's sad face. "Come on, Bernice, we're going home."

Seeing Maggie here in her apartment signals something. There seems to be a space between what she feels and what she thinks. For the past two days she has been thinking about the house at Loon Lake and all the things she felt there. She is no longer afraid of the memories – it was the lag time between thinking about the invasion of her body and her physical response to the memory, she supposes. Bernice knows that she should be feeling: revulsion, fear, anger, resentment.

After any memory, after the thinking, it could take anywhere up to a week (if then) for her to even remember the incident that triggered the emotion. Three in the afternoon Tuesday and she felt a blinding rage that she couldn't even remove herself from or attach to the thought she had had the previous Thursday about her uncle Larry forcing his way into her room, taking all of the life out of her little room under the stairs. The only indication that anything has changed is the quavering in her arms and legs from her anger.

"Shhhhh, *iskwesis*." Freda pats her hand and pulls her comforter around her, mistaking her quaking for cold. She doesn't realize she has called her sistercousin by the diminutive, making her a little girl and not a woman in word and in care. The same cousin who didn't admit the cigarettes she hid in Bernice's coat were hers. The same girl who she heard call her Buffalo Gal behind the Rotary statue of the too large Beaver. The same nearwoman who put her in harm's way with their uncles. This woman, she remembers.

Bernice almost recoils from the touch, old habits die hard, but her face remains impassive.

For inside she is alive. Living through recall. Feeding herself memories. Once, when Bernice was in grade school she was picked to play a snowflake in her class play. One of three snowflakes, she felt certain she could blend in with the other children. However, her outfit, a *papier mâché* costume, was bigger than everyone else's costume. Her mom didn't have enough flour to bind all of the spikes that were supposed to form. After reading and rereading the instructions that Bernice's grade three teacher had written out, her mom had given

Tracey Lindberg

up and gone with her brothers to a neighbour's house to drink. Bernice ran over to Val's, half-damp monstrous confection in her hands, crying all the way. Auntie Val had eventually taken a blow dryer to the mass and made semi-spikes out of toilet paper rolls, which she stapled to the front of the mess. Bernice was horrified to have to pull the soggy heap on her head and dreaded walking in front of the people gathered in the auditorium.

The next night, she and Freda held hands all the way to the schoolyard. Because it was a winter festival, everyone was expected to dress up for pictures and for the party that would follow. Bernice had worn a dress her dad brought back from the Kresge's in Grande Prairie. When she took her coat off and picked up her costume, Penny Rein said, "I have pyjamas that look exactly like that, Bernice the Buffalo." Bernice looked down at her dress, which she now knew absolutely was a nightgown. Waves of shame passed over her as she realized the true nature of her outfit.

"Shhh, Penny," Mrs. Rein warned her daughter. The admonition was worse than the observation. Bernice felt her heart rate multiply. She busied herself putting on her costume, noted Mrs. Rein's grimace, and when the Reins walked away and when she was sure no one was looking at her, she walked back out into the night air. She was halfway home before she realized she had forgotten her winter coat. She continued trudging through the snow, wondering what she would tell her parents. When she got home, the lights were off in the tiny house. Stealthily removing her boots, she tiptoed to the little room under the stairs.

"What're you doin' home?" uncle Larry, whiskey on his breath, snarled from the kitchen – where he would be sitting alone, as always, with a bottle in front of him.

"Nnnothing," she whispered. "I mean, Mmmmom and Auntie Val are coming home soon." She doesn't dare mention Freda, fearing his excitement.

"Nnnnnno, they're nnnnnnot," he mocked her meanly. "Ttthey wwwent tttto tttown twwwo hours ago. Thththth- they will be at the school, llllooooloooolooooking for you."

Her first instinct was to bolt, but something within her, something she will train herself to forget as she grows older- wiser, told her to try to talk him out of his intention.

"Uh uh uncle, I am so tired and sick, I think I am going to throw up or somethin'." He was not sure whether to believe her, angling his large frame between her and her doorway.

"Pppplease, let me go by . . . I need to get my nightgown."

At the mention of her nightclothes he perked up and she pretended not to notice. He did let her by him and she was trapped in her room with his looming figure blocking out the light. "Well, what are you waitin' for, put 'em on." He stood and stared and then, ridiculously, lowered his eyes. She was aware of the ludicrous nature of this moment, of all of these moments. No one mentioned the obvious; no one said what he was waiting for, what she suspected her uncle Aubrey would wait for if Larry was not around. No one talked about it, said a word, made demands, ordered her to do anything. The pure red rage of her seeming complicity – her failure to scream, to speak of this, to fight it, to cry – washed over her. He sensed her pause, perhaps smells her momentary bravery and lunged

Tracey Lindberg

for her. She reached for something, anything to stop him. Tore down the string that turned the overhead light on. And. Off. And then. Nothing but the smell of her own panic and hysteria filling the room.

She didn't talk for a year after. The funny thing is – no one seemed to notice. No one mentioned that her underwear was bloodied, that there were bruises on her arms and neck. No one brought up her swollen lip or the cut above her eyebrow. Once in a while, when the drinks were just starting to pour, someone referred to the Christmas pageant that they'd all shown up at ("Dressed to the nines!") and how the odd biglittle girl from under the stairs simply failed to show up. Like pressure on a bruise, all but Auntie Val pushed slowly to remind her of her failing, of her unreliability. She neither commented on it nor ignored it, and for that year she simply did not hear anything at all. Maggie was barely present in her body, let alone the house, by that time. Bernice was under siege and alone.

Auntie Val sees her. Has always seen her. Notices the rigidity in Bernice's face and her hands clutching the bedclothes in a vise. Deathvise. And. Starts to pray.

acimowin

One day the wolf he comes
Upon this land and he wants to make it his
See, said the Storyteller.
So he runs circles around it again and again
And nothing will grow there
From that day on the wolf,
He bounces like
What is that thing you kids like?
Like a pinball? Yeah, a pinball
Back and forth on his land
Until one day
One tree
One tiny tree
He sees it and it sits in his way
But he sees it too late and smashes into it
That was the end of that wolf
He was too too greedy
Had to have it all

Tracey Lindberg

9

WHAT WAS DONE WAS DONE

wahkewisiw: s/he is vulnerable to sickness

pawatamowin
She dreams an old list.

    pemmican
    moose gut
    deer brain
    Glosettes raisins

S HE WAS JUST TWENTY-FOUR, a baby still really. She had been six years from care and living in Edmonton. One of her cousins had seen her in the Daylight Inn restaurant (which was, ostensibly, Indian tolerant – it let Indian people eat and stay there – but this bred a particular hostility in some of the staff) just off Jasper. She had been to the shelter on 97th Street the night before and had a shower. She imagined she looked like herself, though she rarely felt like Bernice anymore. The word that comes to her is an old one: *kweskatisowin*. It means change of life – not the *moniaw* change of life, but an intricate one that takes root in spirit first and body next. Her *kohkom* had mastered it as a woman, as one who could shift her shape and change her life. But for Bernice, the meaning is different. It's a shifting of yourself in your life. She thought maybe the cousin could see it, but she did not. The cousin was eating a roast beef sandwich. Bernice was nursing a second cup of coffee when she was spotted. The cousin had hugged Bernice, not having seen her in a long time. She, herself, was living in Winnipeg and did not get much news from home. The news she had gotten, however, was good: the band office was putting on a talent show for the *Pimatisewin* and she was driving up there now. Would Bernice like to come?

She had been dreaming about that tree every day. Well, not every day. Sometimes she could not sleep because of that drum group that practised near the shelter. They pounded day and night and Bernice found that the music was soothing, but hard to get out of her head. Also, she kept dreaming about that fat little chef and was worried she had a crush on him that she did not know about. But, she dreamed of that tree so often she thought of him as family.

She had to go. The cousin loaded up Bernice's scant luggage and was polite enough to roll down the windows a bit without mentioning the street smell that her big cousin carried with her, regardless of the shower and Bernice's fastidiousness. Driving out of the city and heading north on the highway they listened to music that Bernice had not heard for years. Merle Haggard, the Carter Family, Patsy Cline. The cousin tried to get Bernice to listen to some newer tunes, but when Bernice did not respond, she put the Georgie Jones CD back in the player.

They drove and listened, stopping for gas at Swan Hills and passing the road map of her childhood. When they got to Grande Prairie, Bernice noticed that it had really grown. On the highway into town there was a Tim Hortons and a Sawridge hotel where the roller rink used to be. Other than that, the hustle of the town sounded and smelled the same. The cousin chattered and ooohed and aaaahed over the changed city, but Bernice knew better. It was the same people, or their children, in the bars, the same hunger just a ways out of town, and the same noiseless sky at night when you turned to head west from Grande Prairie.

Day turned to night as they edged their way out to their community. Being extra-diligent for deer and moose, they slowed down and felt each bump in the roads. From Gibsons, Bernice looks around and she sees twenty-four-year-old Bernice clutching the armrest and soothes her. Cooooo cooooo cooooo.

When they got to the house, the cousin dropping her and

waiting for her to get in, Bernice held her breath. She did not know whether to knock or to just go inside. Freda took that choice out of her hands, pulling the door open and grabbing a hold of her cousin.

"Bernice! I knew you would come! You came for the talent show, right?" Freda was all glitter and short this, sheer that.

"Hello, Freddy," Bernice said shyly.

"Come in, come in, it's gonna snow soon." Freda grabbed the poster tube, the Aer Lingus bag and the garbage bag (which made tinny whines and glassy tinks as she swung it over her shoulder).

Bernice scanned the living room carefully, like a hunter, noted that the gun case was open, there were many bottles on tables and near the door, and that beyond the living room the kitchen looked a mess.

"Tell me, tell me, cuz . . ." – she looked Bernice over and noted her clothes were rumpled and that her hands looked chapped – ". . . whattya been up to?"

Bernice sat herself carefully on the couch. Birdie watches her from her perch at Lola's and sees the way her body transformed from woman to child in that instant.

"Where is. Everyone?" Bernice felt breathless and her heart felt like it was winding up only to release itself and beat even faster.

Something slid across Freda's face, from her eyes to her mouth, something that might have felt like knowledge. "They had sweat and then everyone went to the hall to get it ready for the show. Oh!" she said, animated again. "The uncles went to town for some beer. They won't be back for hours.

Tracey Lindberg

"Let me get you something to . . . get you some tea, Bernice," she said. Bernice said that would be nice and looked around the place she had called home. Got up and locked the door before sitting down and exhaling.

Bird Bernice looked out the window. A single snowflake had fallen.

⎯⎯

It started with a snowflake, Bernice comes to realize. Sure, it likely started in someone else's lifetime, but the beginning of the end started with a stupid snowflake. While Freda made tea, she went to her old room to look for something clean to wear for the talent show. She found a sweater that *Kohkom* Rose had given her with Scotty dogs on the front. It was too small, and the small metal chain that had been drawn from the white dog to the black one had long since stretched, broken, fallen off and been lost. The sweater was part of her old comfort outfit. The bottom was a super-sized pair of old blue jeans.

They were worn through in the knees and were torn and flapped at the ankles. She used to like pulling the sweater over her knees and securing it underneath her feet when she sat on the chair by the front window. Back when the outfit was supposed to give her comfort, she would read a book until it got dark or someone came home. Then, ordinarily, she would go to her room, push her dresser in front of the door and read until she was falling asleep or had to pee.

She remembered that after her Christmas pageant, peeing became a major hassle. She tried to make sure that she didn't drink anything after five o'clock but sometimes, if she was pretending to be a normal kid or if she forgot she was under siege, she would drink something and have to move the dresser, flee to the bathroom, and then listen at the door for pure silence before padding down the hall to her room. Once there, she would push the dresser back into place, sit down and try to regulate her breathing.

On the day of the beginning of the end, Bird Bernice watches the big Cree woman and her tiny cousin as they sat and drank tea. She sees that sheBernice was visibly relieved because everyone had money and, she assumed, was partying, hungover or passed out. She didn't care, as long as they weren't home, where her uncles spent the night. Freda's words flitted and fluttered through the room and let her know that Maggie was staying with Auntie Val, whose diabetes had kept her in her bed in the city for a few days now.

It was just starting to get dark, she remembers. She had unpacked her poster tube and she and Freda were looking at that picture of Jesse and reminiscing just before they started supper. Shots broke the late-afternoon silence. People who had not been paid were hunting seriously to beat the snowfall. She and Freda teased each other back and forth. Freda teased Bernice about how long her hair was becoming and Bernice teased her about her latest Phil (this time, it was Little Joe Mayville, a long-time neighbour and admirer). The hamburgers were almost ready when Freda exclaimed, "Snow, Bernice, I saw a piece of snow!"

"What? Can't be, there hasn't even been frost yet!" And then, with dread, "Oh Freda, we have to close the sweat."

Tracey Lindberg

"Can't it wait until uncles come home?" Freda asked.

She looked at her, in the way *Kohkom* Rose looked at her when she was asking too many questions.

"Okay, okay, let's just see if there's . . ."

"No, don't unlock . . ." Too late. Uncle Larry was just walking in at that moment and caught the door as Freda opened it.

She and uncle stared at each other. She knew that look. And. Then. He looked drunkenly at Freda. Bernice felt ill. She knew that look, too. The one before the one he just gave her. Freda looked nervously back and forth between them. She had her own look. Birdie remembers it. That look she had when Bernice got heck for having her skinny cousin's cigarettes. The look said, "Not me, not me, not me."

"Get out, Freda."

"Awww, Bernice, I just wanna . . ."

"Now." She realized she was almost yelling. "Get your coat and run to the gas station."

Uncle staggered to block Freda but she was small and not paralyzed by the fear to which Bernice had grown accustomed. She had her shoes on before he could reach her; Freda grabbed her coat and ran to the side door.

"Bernice . . ." She stood ten feet away from the house, and looked at her cousin with wide eyes.

"Go Freda. Go." She pushed roughly past uncle and closed and locked the door.

Her birdself watches. And. Waits.

❧

Get away from me, dirty old man. She thought she said it, but it was hard to know. Everything, in her mind, was happening at 7/8ths speed. Sort of like when you just slowed down a record a bit by lightly weighting it with your finger. It made sense, it just wasn't quite regular.

Not again. Never again. She was not sure if she said that, but she does know that she said this, "You want to be sure about this."

Through clenched teeth and with similar fists.

The tremor that had been visiting her for months now, almost like a chatter from the cold, was conspicuously absent. She also knew that her movements seemed steady, although that may have been in comparison with the uncle's movements. He seemed jerky and agitated, and she would like to say that he was not there, that she could not see him, but she could. He was in there somewhere, behind the smell of whiskey and the reek of cigarettes, peeking from behind something that shared a shadow with fear. Maybe it was birdher's eyes but it seemed that, for once, she could Now see him/bravadohim, perhaps even saw him Then, as he really was. He said something about liking a fighter and, repulsed as she was, she almost laughed. Instead, it sounded like a choke or a wheeze from deep within her. Of course he liked a fighter. But he loved passivity more. He thrived in her silence. She thought, in a flash, she needed to be silent tonight.

One last time.

"Where you goin', my girl?" uncle says to Freda, minutes gone. It is the dearness of the phrase, the sick understanding of what the *my* means. The resemblance between uncle

Tracey Lindberg

and Freda clear, only in that instant. Freda's paternity. The link. Between Freda and the family. This. This as much as his wheeze, "C'mere little Bernice. C'mere you sweet thing. Did you miss your old uncle?" Changes her.

For a long time, since it started, she pretended that her uncle was not an uncle when he did this, that he shape-shifted and became something less than uncle and more than animal. She had also assumed that when he shifted, his vision was blurred and she was no longer Bernice, just a body. Now she knew, as she saw him behind his eyes and heard her name, that he was just uncle. Not a wolf. Not a man. And he was bad.

She remembered, in that glint of his eye, him playing fiddle and devilishly jigging around all of the women in the room at dances and gatherings. Sitting for hours at the kitchen table, telling stories and laughing, black hank of hair twisted over his eye like Elvis. And later. Other dances. Walking like a child getting off of the tilt-a-whirl. Other tables. Slamming fists and shouting. His mean mouth and menace aimed at Maggie with seemingly no impetus. The distance her mother and the aunties created between uncle and the girls. Uncle and themselves. And now all she saw was a lecherous old man, still muscular and quick, for he was now in his fifties, heading towards her with a mixture of malice and something that her mind processed as desire.

Bernice had watched enough TV to know that it was possible for someone to "snap." When one's mind snapped, it was thought to signal the beginning – of a new consciousness, of a new behaviour, of a new personality. Watching *NYPD Blue* and *Law and Order* had taught her that. When it happened to her, however, snapping was the sign of the end. Like the closing of a book, if you will, her ability to numb herself to what the uncle did was closed. No longer able to harden herself, to forgive him this trespass, to will herself to forget every day after, her eyes were wide open. Her nerve endings were alive and her muscles were taut.

Watching herself from her Bird's-eye view in Gibsons her body is similarly ready for attack.

Snap. Snap. Snap (like the fingers in *West Side Story* when the rival gangs meet). He walked towards her, unsteadily, but not unsure.

Snap. Snap. Snap (like twigs being walked on late in the fall). She saw his left arm rise towards her head and his right arm move towards her chest.

Snap. Snap. Snap (she sidestepped him and he lurched forward, running into the living room wall by the door). She flew across the room, airborne and graceful. She heard the air in his chest release and imagined his anxiousness rising in him like a helium-filled balloon.

Snap. Snap. Snap (she grabbed for something, caught air, which birdshe notices magically became the uncle's work boot). He placed his hands on the wall and slid down to his knees.

Snap. Snap. Snap (hands raised effortlessly with the leather footwear, a coloured rainbow arcs as she swung the steel-toed boot through the air). She stopped at the last instant, aware that he was not moving and was continuing his slide to the floor.

Snap. Snap. Snap (neurons flashed and hissed and sent the message to her arm from her brain). Heart attack. Uncle has had a heart attack.

There was no relief, only revulsion, at the realization that this excitement had overwhelmed him. She wanted him to look up at her and plead with teary eyes for help, forgiveness, silence. But he is only gasping when a particularly horrible screamwheeze was leaving his lungs. "Save me, Birdie."

BirdBernice pays particular attention. She has never seen this, never remembered this before. She is rapt under her comforter.

Snap. Snap. Snap (old matches on an old matchbook striking ineffectually). "Creator, give me a sign," she had prayed. The uncle stared at her. They lit. She threw the matches, picked up her stuff (in the picture, Jesse is looking at her with foreboding, heavy-lidded) and walked slowly to the door.

"Save yourself," she said.

She is not sure how long she stood there, watching. She struggled with the poster tube, pictures and her makeshift luggage. Put on her coat and walked outside. Birdshe wills her to turn around, to see what she forgot. She does, slowly. The match must have taken immediately as the curtains were already on fire by the window where he fell down. She walked away. She must have stood there for some time, for when she looked down she saw that her hands were blistered. Could feel her feet burning. Wonders absently how long she stood there. Walked. To the hill and the old tree. It had no life in it.

She remembers.

acimowin

The Storyteller guffawed
That Wolf!
Never did learn his lesson
He wanted the taste of owl in his
mouth
Every time he saw her
The wolf ran around
her, sniffing and leering, wondering
what she looked like without skin on
She looked at his crazy eyes and wondered
about the strength of her beak.

Tracey Lindberg

10

SHE WRITES HER OWN STORY

omekinawew: one who shares food

pawatamowin
There is noise below her, and she is afraid she will wake while in the air. She looks down and sees a raven, an eagle and an old mangy crow eating KFC.

AUNTIE VAL

VALENE STARTS CRYING AND CANNOT STOP; only sleep calms her. When she wakes up, the frozen face and clenched hands of her niece behind her in the night, the papers are gone and Bernice lies, dressed and groomed, and seemingly asleep in her freshly made bed.

There is something written on one single paper on the table and it seems to be in Val's own handwriting:

Pasakoskow[*]
Amiskowiyâs[†]
Maskekewapoy[‡]

And. She isn't sure, but she thinks one of her cigarettes is missing.

Bernice lies in the bed. In wait? In the quiet. Every so often, Val tells her a story, sings her a song or holds her hand as she prays. Birdie's hands are soft from the lard and butter and they feel remarkably strong for a womangirl who has been wasting in her bed for weeks. She has held these hands since Bernice was an infant, staring at her, puckered and red-faced, her tiny cleft palate gleaming like the inside of an oyster shell. She was always a big kid. She was a big baby. She and Maggie used to open their eyes wide at each other over little Birdie's big head. Part in wonder that such a big child had come from such a tiny

---

[*] Sticky spruce gum.

[†] Beaver meat.

[‡] Medicine water or medicine tea.

Tracey Lindberg

woman. Part in complicit acceptance of some unspoken and silent deal they made never to talk about those hard months before the birth. Births.

She realizes that underneath all of that flesh, all of that Bernice, all of that protective armour, Bernice exists as a tiny replica of Maggie. Val finds this disconcerting as the *kee kuh wee sis* to her littlebig girl. Bernice no longer looks like her.

Valene Meetoos has always been the big woman in the room. In her twenties and thirties she came into that. Raised by a good woman and a good man, she came to expect greatness from herself and was quite seldom let down. When she turned forty and discovered she had "the goddamned diabetes" she became more aware of her diet. She also began to look around and see the potential for the sickness around her. Always close to Bernice and her other nieces and nephews, she began to notice that the girls were hiding. With some it was in the wide open – big heels, makeup and tight pants – but with Bernice it was different. Maybe she noticed more because Bernice looked just like her, but larger, but Bernice was hiding more in books and food than Val was comfortable with. In her tiny little hutch, like a big caged rabbit, Bernice would stock all manner of food and literature.

That place was a firetrap anyhow, Valene thinks.

When her brother died, and later still when her sister left, Valene mourned as if they were saints because that was the only way she was going to be able to forgive herself when her time came. She would mourn Bernice the same way if something should happen. "Something should happen" would be starvation or dehydration, she imagines.

When Bernice was little, when Bernice was young, she could write and tell such stories. You could not shut her up. When Val would visit, she would sit on the tiny bed under the stairs and listen to her niece, really her daughter from another mother, tell stories of princesses, crazy dogs and travels that were full and rich in their detail. Val would bring all of her new boyfriends to meet her fantastic niece as soon as she thought they might be around for more than a month. Unfailingly, the newly ex-boyfriends would end up as badmen or monsters in the next instalment of Bernice's tales.

When Bernice was in her early teens and Valene was thirty they shared space while Bernice went to that Christly place. Valene noticed, in the beginning, when she could notice, that it became harder and harder to coax her niece out of her shell. Stories had to be pulled from her. Family didn't appear in stories except as bit characters. She often wondered if this was because Maggie had gone off again – no stopping in town to see her sister and daughter as she tried to make herself disappear, bit by bit. Even so, and every so often, the villains sounded vaguely familiar. Because she had been fighting her dual nature for most of her life, Valene assumed the worst – the worst being the worst thing she could imagine (having intimately experienced mental illness).

When she was just past the age where you can go bra-less (although, by Freda's math, there is no such age), she took Bernice to bingo and a movie and was surprised when Bernice would not leave the truck for two hours. Coaxing, chiding and threatening did not move the girl. Only when Valene promised her movie popcorn and a chocolate bar did her niece leave the vehicle. After that, and it was kind of a blur for Valene as she entered the "bad days," she seemed to remember her daughterniece leaving. The room, the house, her space, her mind – there was a period when all Valene saw was Bernice walking away. (That she, herself, had left her niece alone in an apartment resulting in her going to foster care is not something that Valene can think about. Then. It was too little. Now. It is too much.)

She remembers the last time she saw Bernice walking away. Val had been to the San to visit her, right after the spring ceremonies. Birdie was wrapped in bandages and stared at her blankly. She didn't utter a word until she had turned around to go back to her room.

"*Pimatisewin*," she whispered.

The look in her eyes was not what bothered Valene. After four years of living in Edmonton (under Edmonton, about Edmonton?), her niece had taken on a look that shook Valene: Bernice had the wariness and walk of a street person. Assured and confident with a whisper of scary. She wonders when that happened – was she wary before she ran to Edmonton? Was she cautious before that, with that white couple? Had she developed that look, most bothersome, when Valene was supposed to be on watch? When those Christly nuns tried to own her? Or, was it sometime earlier, at Loon, Bernice fighting for survival – as generations of Meetoos women had – from uncles? Valene feels like she is excavating a pain dig, watching a car crash in reverse.

Valene stares at Bernice hardsoftly. She is not resting. She is not in peace. But. She has most certainly left the building.

The thought shakes her, but she has comfort in the fact that her daughterniece has not stirred, not moaned, not tensed any muscle in days. She hears Lola and Freda bickering from downstairs. *It's just sugar and flour for pete's sake, what on earth could they find to argue about every day?*

Looking at her watch and turning on the TV, she takes her leave from her Bernice and says a prayer to Creator for her. Remembering, she grabs the list of medicines, shakes her head and wanders downstairs to see how those skinny cronies are doing.

LOLA

Lola catches herself staring at Freddy again. Stops. Looks at what she is doing. She has been invoicing the Ramada for all of the fresh-baked goods they provided last week. Their regular baking company is on strike and Freda, Lola and Val have made a killing – and almost killed each other – preparing huge batches day and night for a convention in town.

Say whatcha want about their men, but their women are the hardest workers I've seen, she thinks, not even aware of who the they really is. When she talks about we and they, it is almost always in terms of men and women, and that the women who now live above her business most probably see her as "them" would never occur to her.

Valene comes down and puts the kettle on, asking if anyone else wants tea? All three do. Lola puts down her billing, Freda stops doing dishes and Val sets out cups for them as the water starts to boil. Lola has come to love this. Well, not love, you can't love anything when The Kid is up there . . . doing whatever she is doing. But, she likes to sit with these two women (one her younger browner reflection and the other an inverted funhouse version of herself) and take them in. She has never seen so many Indians up close before and she is mostly surprised that they are pretty much like her. Well, they don't talk much and they think a lot more, and they tend to communicate through some sort of shorthand that she can't quite figure out. Otherwise? Just like her, she thinks.

"Anybody want a b-b-b-brownie?" she stutters, afraid of giving offence.

Val and Freda, who have never been called or considered themselves "brownies" in their lives, hide smiles. Then grins. And then, Freda breaks: "Fuck it. You old racist," she says, squeezing Lola's hand and laughing so hard that the table quivers. When Valene gives in to her own laughter, the table is bumping along with her big belly in a happy thump thump thump. Lola doesn't understand and is just so relieved not to have been the asshole at the table, and quite affected by Freda's touch, that she laughs along.

"Yes or no, brownies?"

"Yes, yes, Lola, please," Valene says, gasping.

She walks to the backroom. *Odd ducks*, she thinks, laughing her quack-like laugh.

She thinks to herself that she should take those two out some night; maybe let Margo sit with The Kid. All of 'em dressed in finery, just some broads leaving their trouble behind for a few hours.

Lola goes to a karaoke bar around the corner from the bakery once a month. With her pint-sized skintight clothes and her heartfelt delivery of Patsy Cline songs she has become something of a celebrity, in that nasty way that noto-riety and contemptuous familiarity are sometimes celebrated. She always writes her name on twenty slips and when her name is called there are hoots and hollers from regulars and irregulars alike. Maybe it is her sheer blouse, perhaps it is her thigh-high skirt or her follow-me-and-fuck-me heels, but the overdressed and overly rambunctious woman is enjoying a sort of anti-popularity each time she goes there.

That a craggy old baker should be singing Patsy Cline in Gibsons, British Columbia, did not strike her as one bit odd. That she was there when one Mr. Pat John, television star, took the stage did not even give her pause. He looked bigger than she remembered. He was travelling with a unibrowed white friend and a seemingly ever-present blonde, accepting congratulations and apparent admiration for a career mostly forgotten. Lola knew something about Jesse that she did not know about herself: he was an oddity at the bar, something to break up the space between finishing one drink and ordering another. On this particular night she was sitting half on and off some no-account's lap, earning free Harvey Wallbangers, when in walked Mr. Television Indian himself.

His obliging and obligatory blonde seemed uninterested in his stories. The less attention she paid, the larger his gestures became. He wanted to occupy all the space in the tiny lounge and it seemed he was uncomfortable in his skin. He had one hanger-on – Lola thinks that the guy probably used to be part of an entourage and that he looked a little embarrassed to be part of this nearly-anonymous-and-not-wanting-to-be three-some.

For a while she was oblivious because the no-account cheapskate sitting under her felt a score coming on and started to buy her drinks in earnest. She squirmed on no-account's lap to keep him involved and then slurexcused herself to go to the washroom. On the way she met the blonde's eyes, who rolled them – whether at being Jesse's date, at the sight of a drunken oldish woman in a too-short spandex skirt and high-heeled red cowboy boots, or at their shared occupation that evening, Lola was unsure.

When she walked out of the bathroom she ran into entourage man. "Hey, is that the *Beachcombers* guy?" she half shouted over someone's version of "Riders On the Storm."

Obviously uncomfortable, Entourage Guy sidestepped her and his reply was muffled as he turned to take a request slip to the DJ booth. She followed him to the booth. "I didn't hear ya," she half yelled at him. "Is that him or not?" She passed the DJ her slip.

"Yeah, that's him. Stick around, he's going to sing in a minute." He walked away, suave in a cheap suit. Something about him yelled out hungry, but the starving can never see beyond their own craving.

She and the DJ looked at each other smugly. When he read her slip he said, "Hey, someone's already singing this one, you'll have to pick another one."

"What? Nobody ever sings that one!" Lola said indignantly, coveting what she considers her song. She scribbled:

Anything by Reba McIntyre.

For effect, she adds:

ANYTHING!

Behind her, the opening chords to her song began. When she turned she saw that Pat John was about to sing the song she had selected. Angrily, she grabbed Pat John's slip and put it in her pocket. It wasn't until the next morning that she found it, crumpled and nearly illegible.

"What the hell?" she said, reading it.

Moose intestine
Oolichan grease
Chokecherry pits

Lola can hear those low murmurs coming from the storefront and she wonders if she should tell the story to Freda and Val. The Kid seemed to like that guy, though, and in a surge of gentleness for them she finds that she doesn't want to tell them anything that reminds them of The Kid in a better state and decides not to bring them anything that costs them. And, they were having a nice time this morning, even if she didn't know what was so funny. Lost in that thought, she burns her thumb on the brownies, cursing as she digs them out and plates them, heading to the storefront.

FREDA

Freda wipes the countertop in the restaurant with vinegar and water. The old bird has started making noises that she is too old to run the place herself and Freda is getting antsy in the attic apartment. So, they walk by each other all day, eat supper together and then pay Bernice and Valene a visit.

It was Lola who had pointed out that Bernice wore a different shirt each day. At first. She makes a mental note to ask Val if she is changing her. Bernice has lost so much weight that Freda and Lola went out and bought her some new tops, thinking that Bernice might want something that fit comfortably. Sometimes when Freda passes those clothes sitting on the tiny dresser, she harrumphs in Bernice's general direction. Impatient with their tidiness, angry with their newness.

Now. They sit there. Washed but unused. Freda is scared to figure out when the shirt became the same shirt. When the San pants became the only pants. The tops are colourful and vivid, clothes Bernice would never choose herself. They are the types of shirts that a girl of eighteen should wear. Well, not Bernice or Auntie Val (who would not make her wear the new clothes), but certainly Lola and Freda at eighteen.

When Freda was girlish, she fancied herself a snappy dresser. Having seen the girls in Vancouver on the way to Gibsons, she knows she was not. It never bothered her before. Dressing provocatively on a budget had always garnered a certain type of attention, and Freda liked it. She saw Lola looking admiringly at a woman dressed in loose and well-cut clothes when they snuck off to the city to get supplies for the bakery one day. Lola caught her staring at the woman and Freda knew in that awkward moment that she had been dressing for a different kind of life, her whole life. Her prom dress (well, she didn't actually graduate, but she did go to the prom with Winston Nighttraveller) was a pink confection. Maggie had started sewing it but became upset one night when she had to remove the gathers from the slippery fabric one too many times. Eventually, they took the dress to a seamstress in Grande Prairie who finished it two hours before the graduation ceremony. Freda remembers the dress. And sometimes, when she allows herself, she recalls Winston's hand on the small of her back, shaking at their proximity. That was then. Before she met her first husband, Louis. Five years after she graduated from girl to woman. Louis used to like it when she dressed in heels and miniskirts. For five years she bent her back out of shape and wondered if her ass was hanging out every time she walked down the street. At first, he would whistle slowly and a lovely light came into his pale-blue eyes when he saw her walking towards him. Later, that lovely light metastasized into a fierce gleam as griefanger replaced tenderness.

Then came a year of sack dresses and stretchy pants as Louis regrouped and she hoped for the glimmer of that light and a smile not so tight again.

She still has the last note she sent to him, and then took back after he had read it and fallen asleep over too many beers at the kitchen table.

Louis,
Where have you gone? Who replaced you with this sad
angry guy? I think you forget that she was my daughter,
too. Do you remember, at the beginning when you told me
you would never hurt me? Not loving me is hurting me too.
Not looking at me and telling me I'm special is lying, too.

Where have you gone?
I am leaving.
Freddy

p.s. I want my money back.

When Freda buys lottery tickets, goes to bingo or plays
poker she puts that note on the table and taps it four times before
making any decision. Maybe she will win back that money that
he took from her underwear drawer when he left. That money
was their daughter's. Money saved for a trip to Disneyland
that she would never take. Money saved for a school she would
never go to. Crinkled bills in a baggie, stashed away. Disease
doesn't care what plans you have, she thought later, you can
have bags of money and your own ideas about what is going
to happen. Doesn't matter. Sickness has its own baggies that it
leaves behind. A stash of rage. A freezer-size bag of unrelent-
ing hurt, one of tears and a garbage bag of plans.

After she left, she went back to wearing miniskirts and
stilettos for a while. Soon, her back was aching again and her
ass dropped. That was the goddamn shame of it – as soon as

she was feeling good enough to wear her cheap and cheery outfits, the bottom fell out.

Still, she wanted to wear those clothes – sheer, high-cut, low-cut, backless, sleeveless (what was left?) – she had wanted to wear them for herself. Not Winston. Not for any white guy. And then. She met Wes Wiebe. Who could have known when Freda fell, really tumbled, it would be for a Phil? She met him at a bar in Edmonton during the rodeo. Black hair and blue eyes, wow, there was something about that combination that did her in every time.

And that time. Oh Lord, sometimes she still gets dizzy just thinking about him. And the way he walked towards her. Asked her to dance and took her hand and led her to the already wet dance floor. Among the beer ruins they slipped and slid together and apart. Two-stepped to country rock. Waltzed to two-steps. Fumbled their clothes off in his old pickup and moved together and apart on horse blankets and Robin's Doughnuts coffee cups.

Four weekends in a row they met and left the bar as soon as they saw each other. Four Fridays and four Saturdays they had near-drunken expressions on their faces as they looked at each other in shock in the glow of the dashboard. Sometimes she remembers the point where he was breathless and teary, and she responded in the same way, as fear and joy dripped from her mouth in a babble of affection plus. In later years, she will wonder if the baggie of her diseased love was the same as his, or if he actually felt those things. Whether she remembered it in a way that made her feel less shameful in what she gave him. Or, rather, gave away.

She worked at a gas station then, and as she remembers it,

work became effortless. The clients less hostile. The demands less demanding. She began to listen to the radio and really heard and understood what all the love songs were about. Humming and sighing, she made her way through the week to sit impatiently and so patiently on a barstool at a seedy country bar in the industrial area of Edmonton. Anticipation battled expectation for supremacy in her belly. And each time, until the last time, she was rewarded with the glimmer of recognition, hope and appreciation in Wes Wiebe's eyes.

Until the last time. After a double shift, a whirlwind of get-ready and a shot of rye to calm her nerves, she sat im/patiently at "their" spot. She had arrived two hours later than usual and was giddy to see the frustration and wanting on her man's face. Glancing under her weekend eyelashes at the door, her hopes rose and fell each time she saw a black cowboy hat. Finally, her fear got the best of her and she started drinking to calm her jangly nerves. She thought about calling him and remembered their playful exchange of the weekend before when she had asked for his telephone number.

Her eyes sting with the sheer shame of it, but she tells herself it's the vinegar she is using to clean the countertops and tells Lola she is heading outside for a smoke.

Her cheeks still burning, she remembers: "I don't have a phone," he teased her, and then kissed the thought from her head. She blushes again thinking of what he wrote on the paper with the pen she had forced on him:

Six pack of Pilsner
Bag of Cheezies

She knows it is stupid, but she kept that note, too. Carries it with her every day. Of course, she now knows with certainty the moment when she unlocked the gate and let her stupidity out. The liquor lubricated her brain, quite opposite of the effect she was hoping for, and her synapses made connections she had talked herself out of. Before. When he was with her. As she got drunker, her folly played out in her head.

"I'm too busy for a girlfriend."

"I only come to town on weekends."

"Tell me where you work, so I'll always know where to find you."

"We've got a good thing here, why ruin it with commitment?"

"I would love to end up with a girl just like you."

"Don't you have other friends who you can hang out with?"

"Maybe you could meet me outside the bar?"

"They're not really my friends; don't pay any attention to them."

And when they said goodbye, always: "Nice knowin' ya."

She didn't know, really didn't understand his cruelty, until the Canadian Club clarified it completely.

That roughness in his mouth extended to his hands and she recognized now that her bruised breasts and scraped thighs were something more than passion. Less than passionate.

And she had responded in kind. Bruising his shoulders, scraping his back. She had thought it was love and had given in to that part of herself that wanted to be hurt. And that piece of the hope of something bigger, something loving, turned into a kernel of something indescribably hard. She wonders now how desperate she must have been to accept that ugly gift and return it. To have felt aroused at the near-beating. At that moment, she began to reject and loathe that thing in her that needed to be hit, hard. And she knew within that fury that she hated him, too. For introducing it so glibly. For making her a one-time offer.

That last night, as her legs got wobblier and her head fuzzier, she began to crave regular, to unkink herself. She undid her shirt to her navel, small brown breasts peeking out every time she almost fell off her chair. She spread her legs lasciviously on the barstool in an open invitation to all the normal men at Cowboys. The man she ended up with was surprised by her lack of responsiveness, and why not, put off by her prudishness.

"Gimme your phone number," she had cried in the middle of the night to the long-empty room.

She showed up at Cowboys for the next four weekends, hoped not to see Wes, prayed that he would show up. And hated herself for needing him. Needing it. Again. Still.

She started wearing stretchy pants again then, wears them to this day, with long sweaters and vivid tops and high heels with the skinniest of heels. It is almost too hot for her clothes in Gibsons, in a week or two she will have to think about shorts and T-shirts. Possibly, she could wear those new tops of Bernice's if her cousin doesn't take a liking to them. Or. Doesn't. She walks into the heat of the bakery, muttering. "Pilsner and Cheezies. Jesus Christ."

She sometimes thinks that she was raised by good women and educated by less than good men. Bernice was one of those good women. She took care of Freda, made sure doors were locked, that Freda had a ride, that she got out safe. Her cousin protected Freda from the uncles. Without knowing that Freda was doubly in jeopardy, more at risk for an unkind life than even Bernice. She loves her cousin dearly for protecting her, even without knowing the uncles' particular interest in her.

Pausing at the doorframe, she is sure she hears that crazy fat wheezing cook in the storefront of the bakery. She looks around, sees Lola sitting in the front window, staring, and goes to look at the ovens. There are pies in the new oven and bread in the old one – it gets and stays hot faster and is better for the loaves that seem to multiply in it. There is an odd smell in the bread oven, something familiar mingles with something she recognizes but does not know well. It smells like the ceremony soup. *Iskwesisihkan.** And something else. Tamarind? She doesn't know the taste, but the smell is like something she tried at one of those Indian buffets Birdie sometimes made her go to. She goes to ask Lola about it, thinks better of it and heads up the stairs, careful not to alert her cousin to her presence. She feels guilty about her stealth. Rather, she thinks she should feel guilty about her stealth. Not wanting to face Bernice or Lola with all of this Wes around her, she hits the top of the stairs. Stops. Gathers herself and walks in to see her cousin. Valene had driven to the city hours ago, telling Lola and Freda she was "getting Birdie's groceries." The big woman had a list in her hand and determination in her eye as she walked out the door. Freda knew better than to say anything, but suspects the list was not her aunt's. But Bernice's. Which is ridiculous. But it has been a while since she believed in reason, anyhow.

* Barley.

Tracey Lindberg

Bernice is on her side, facing away from the door. Her breath is regular, but a bit ragged at the end. Freda feels something heavy in her throat and is surprised to find she is about to cry.

Freda never cries.

She didn't cry when she found out she was adopted. She didn't shed a tear when someone mean told her that she was related by awful birth to Maggie and Val. Didn't spill a drop, not on one day, that she was a "throwaway" baby. Not one salty smattering when her uncles tried to get a hold of her. Not one piece of sadness given over to the knowledge that she was conceived by her uncle's hideous act. Maybe she didn't cry because tears were a currency in her life for so long that holding them back meant she was richer. Whatever the reason, looking at her biglittle cousin, the one who gave up her lifebody so Freda could have her own, she is filled with sadness and pain that she cannot pinpoint, could not describe and will not share. And there is something else. Twin sisters, remorse and regret, sitting next to the ugly cousin at the wake: responsibility.

Freda thinks Birdie is dying. But she also knows she is cooking something up in that head of hers.

That kid never wasted a thought, she says to herself. Stops. Because she sounds like Lola.

acimowin

Oh, this is a good one
the Storyteller says,
Slapping his hand on his thigh at the memory.
The owl loved mice.
She ate and ate mice until
She couldn't move no more and her
Old enemy the wolf, seeing her there
All full
Pounced on her and ate her
He was so full he could only
Shake his head when the
Crow came to peck at him.
The owl she was dead but
So was the wolf
Because that crow ate at him
Until she reached the owl and let her out.
That's why they say
A bird in the belly
Is worth two in the bush.
Hyuh!

Tracey Lindberg

11

THE LAST TRAVEL BEFORE THE FINAL DESTINATION

nakipayiw: s/he stops travelling, s/he stops driving

pawatamowin

She dreams she was home, looking at the burnt-out shell of her uncle's place. Walking a circle around the place where her family is buried. And one time, seeing her father walk by her, glancing quickly at her like he can tell she was there, and then looking at the ground again.

S HE LEFT THE SAN. No one tried to stop her, so she guessed it was okay.

Eventually, she had hitched from Edmonton to Calgary. It was so close to Edmonton – but she had never been. In the end, she couldn't stand that city. Everyone was so snooty there. Even the street women – the hookers had fur coats! That's one story she never told anyone. She didn't think her mom or *Kohkom* would like that she knew that. Bernice stayed there only two days – the place just had a feel of soon-to-be nasty. Like when Skinny Freda got drunk – she looked good and all on the outside but by the time you realize she's gonna be trouble, it's already too late – someone is gonna get hurt. That's what Calgary felt like to Bernice. That and there were too many cowboys and not enough Indians. People stared at her. Her fat. Her scars (healed but angry). She thought they could smell the San on her.

She wanted to see more people who looked like her, so she hopped in a big rig for a ride to Lethbridge. It was just a stop on the way to Waterton Park – and she wants to see the trees that the Blackfoot use in their ceremonies. It is ironic that she paid for the ceremony in ways that were unceremoniously troubling. She's not proud of how she paid her way, but something was expected and she only had what she had. Anyway – it didn't mean much to her – she had done worse than that before. That trucker – he was real stinky, though, smelled like ass and hair. Smart as a whip, when she tried to boost his wallet he smacked her, not so hard though, and gave her a twenty and the bottle they were drinking from. That asshole dropped her off in front of the cop shop – like she would have been able to walk with the bottle unnoticed in Lethbridge, Alberta.

The first thing she took in about that place was the old people – lots and lots of old white people. Another thing she saw was big Indians. They're Bloods there – really tall. She was not used to that – other than her *Moshom* she had never seen a tall Indian.

Maybe they aren't tall and just feel that way, she had thought at the time. *Bush Crees – we're usually small for hunting and running. These Bloods – some of the women are almost six feet! Not so friendly either – one woman looked me up and down like a white guy. No wonder the Bloods and Crees don't get along, we are two different people.*

An old Blood couple had given her a ride to Waterton, though. They were really nice people – asking about her family and all. She hadn't wanted to lie to them, they were so kind, so she just pretended she couldn't hear. They talked all the way though, all about their kids and grandchildren. Just like Bernice's *Moshom* and *Kohkom* – talk of the young ones filled the air around them. Those old Bloods lived right near the big national park – still their traditional territory, they said – so they didn't mind taking Bernice right to the gate. It was April then so there was no one sitting at the gate and thank goodness, because she needed those twenty dollars.

The whole way there she just stared at those mountains. Coming from the north, the prettiest thing to her is the bush and the lakes; she had no idea what this *bigness* was. The rocks were big – bigger than anything she had ever seen. And the mountains pushed up into the sky so at some points you couldn't even see the blue past the hulk of the mountains blocking out the sky. Her first day there she just walked and walked – she didn't even get back into the town until night-fall because there was so much to see. She wished she had a camera because she wanted that picture – blue sky caress-ing mountain of stone – to always be as beautiful to her as it appeared in that moment. Sometimes when you see some-thing every day you forget its mystery and she wanted to keep this place as hers, as it appeared that day. She started think-ing about the wildflowers near her old house and how she couldn't remember what they looked like and that hurt so she just kept walking. She knew the bears were just waking up but wasn't scared. She made sure that she didn't go near the medicines growing in the bush and kept mostly near the road – she heard the hum of traffic once in a while.

She had come upon a little set of falls, fat and furious with spring runoff, and found a little rock that said "god is love" near the side of the falling water.

In a couple of weeks, when it got really warm, no one would be able to see that little rock because of the runoff and she felt sad for herself because she was the last one to carry the message and she knew there was no love. As much as Bernice hated feeling sad and pitiful, the wave of pain came upon her so quickly that she couldn't avoid it.

And then the stone people had talked to her, but she was trying to forget their talk – it hurt too much to be away from home and she didn't want to hear their tongue. She could hear the spirittalk from the rock and felt blessed that she knew the language that so many had forgotten. They told her that

Maggie was gone. She didn't listen to that news then, could not absorb the weight of the meaning, but she can still feel the full weight of all they have lost, as a family, sitting at the side of the bed, patiently waiting for her to receive it. At the time she thought the ache it caused would be too much, and that it might turn her to stone, too. She had tried to convince herself, there in the stone and sitting in the richness of the company of the stone people, that her mind was playing tricks on her. She can feel Maggie's absence in the bakery because it wafts from her cousin and her aunt, too.

She wishes she had all that stone around her now, wishes she had asked the stone people questions. Instead, she had soothed herself. She sang a little song, a children's walking song, and went to a lake with no one around her for miles. She had pulled out a photocopied picture of Jesse from her bag and put it in the soil as an offering to say thanks for her journey, but with the booze in her jacket it didn't feel quite right. She decided right then and there to get rid of it. Drinking it was hard, but she had lots of practice, so she just opened her throat and poured.

After that she wandered around a bit before she could find the road. Around seven o'clock Bernice found the little town again – it wasn't so difficult – you just walk downhill and eventually you come upon it.

The next day, after her third dirty look from the park ranger, she decided to head west again and hitched a ride to Vancouver. Sometime she will write a book about that. Lola said one time that her stories could turn a whore to blushing.

When the truck driver dropped her off at a shelter, she

checked in, and felt the absence of life, of soil, of nature. As soon as she recognized the feeling, she went to the flower store on the corner. They must have thought she was crazy. Didn't buy anything, really couldn't afford it. She had just stood by the glass cases, never opening them, and imagined the smell. Sure, she knew it wouldn't be the same. Still, it was comforting to think that these flowers came from fields and old *kohkoms'* gardens. The self-delusion was important. She caught herself pressing her face against the glass, the humming of the flower fridge grounded her. She had to leave quickly, people were staring. After that, she couldn't get the scent out of her head. Walking to the alley, not quite sure what she was looking for, she opened the lid of a huge blue bin. The smell of rotting and mildewing flowers took her breath away. On the tip of her tongue came a word she had never heard: death-garden.

And then she saw it. A semi-bouquet of wilting tiger lilies. You could pick them back home. They were bountiful. People back home tried not to, though, because their smell was fresh even when they were dying – it was better to let them live. To let the smell live. Still, her momma used to let her pick them from beside the house. They would pull them out in bunches, throwing them in old Planters peanut jars and baking soda cans. It was like they had a treasure, a secret garden that no one on the outside of their home could imagine. Giddy, they would laugh and tell stories about the old days when grand-mothers would swat at their kids, and smiled at the same time at their ingenuity.

In an alley, in a coastal city, where she knew no one, she jumped in, grabbed the damp bouquet, imagining their smell and touch. Played with their parts. She put them in her jacket and crawled awkwardly out of the trash bin. Two old ladies had stared at her, like she was a maniac or something.

Running to the shelter, climbing up the stairs, she could hardly wait to get them in water. Her hands were shaking, she was so excited. When she opened them up and put them on the table she noticed an odour about them. She breathed in deeply, wanting to pull their soft sweet smell into her toes.

They smelled like dirt.

That smell now lingers in her little loft. After the shelter and after the ride to Gibsons she had lost them to the air, falling out and dropping wherever she passed, one petal at a time. The flowers are long gone and the dirt smell came back just yesterday, but Bernice knows it is there. She is less able to reconcile herself with the recent past, so that the return of the smell surprises her. Now, at Lola's, she is able to see and begin to understand what her past has been while the musty wet smell of earth permeates the tiny rooms like music. Her senses are alive now, no matter what her makeshift family is seeing. She knows things. Feels things. Smells things. Wants to start to believe things. Hears things.

"You were a baby," she hears an owl cry.

"No one deserves this," a whisper.

She is talking to herself.

She does not feel mad, she left the crazy behind when she crawled into bed. She is wondering if the Creator sees her, heard her while she is in this bed, because she was questioning whether he even existed. It had come to her slowly that she has no God. It had first visited her on a Thursday night at some faux-Latino bar in the core of Gibsons' downtown after four gins and when she was on the verge of falling in some guy's lap (no small feat) around last call. The first and last last call.

The thought that came to her then was that she had to take care of herself because there was no one watching out for her anymore.

Then. On her road to Godlessness.

She had left with Some Guy anyway. A second thought came to her that night. When you are this far from God you can be optimistic 'cause you have nothing. She almost pondered it again on the way home in the cab but was struck with the loveliness of being alone with her thoughtlessness.

When she got to Gibsons, Bernice had forced herself out every night for three weeks. If Lola noticed her haggard appearance she did not comment. This was somewhat discomfiting. She had let her hair grow wild – wild like a bush Indian, her *kohkom* would have laughed. Except it was short and entirely grey now. It turned overnight. No one has mentioned it, and Birdie knows they won't. It's understood that she has seen something. Bad. In the dark times, the *Whitigo** comes. Especially when you are sleeping. She didn't let herself sleep much those days but on the one night she did, something changed her hair.

It didn't seem odd to her to believe in evil and to disbelieve in benevolence. Disregard kindness. Distinctly disavow goodness. She had the faith that optimists and pessimists share – it could only get better. Also, there is a crazy tune in her head – her default category song. It sounds familiar and she thinks

* Spirit, a sometimes bad spirit.

Tracey Lindberg

she may have heard it on the radio (97.2 The Fox Rocks) or on the pow wow trail. It was some drum group she vaguely remembered but could not place. But that was then, when she let the madness take the memories. Except now they seem to want back in.

"*Heyaaa heyaaa.*" Crescendo decrescendo. Electric and acoustic. The cadence was sensible – in that she could actually feel the music surge through her.

Somewhere in the recesses of her recess, she knows that when she got to Gibsons she began numbing herself – and for no good reason. For a bad reason, most certainly. Now, she might know that when she started sinking it started outside of her. It was almost like feeling the ground outside of you give – like quicksand – before your insides felt the pressure and responded to the weight of the sand engulfing it. Until the outside shift resulted in the pressure on her insides, she could only feel external stimulation. Self-realization aside, it was really not that easy to live within yourself in public. And so very public.

The second sign that she was free-falling past goodness and Godliness came to her at Lola's birthday party. She threw the old lady a birthday party at Lou's Blue Bayou on Highway 101. It was really an act of love/self-love because she wanted to get the old bird drunk. Getting drunk with strangers was numbing, but seeing someone she knew loaded might allow her to see the sense in sedation. Lola, decked out like the diva she is, was free-spirited and had a pink to her cheek that Bernice had never seen before. Bernice had invited all of "the girls," Lola's Whippet-tongued poker crew.

Everyone had doted on Lola, commented on her hair – newly shorn and dyed red – and her jean jumper, a gift that Bernice had sewn for the occasion. What Bernice did not tell her: she had sewn some sage into the cuffs, women's medicine, to keep Lola well.

Lola had danced with men – young and old – her cooking, karaoke and sharp conversation had made her famous in the small seaside town. She drank bourbon with vigour and toasted herself regularly throughout the evening. Bernice brought out her outside self, which she always did when she had to be seen.

Her outside self drank gin. Too much gin. She, too, danced with men young and old, although with fewer than Lola and the Whippets. And toasted Lola regularly. And skirted from conversation to conversation with ease. She can see her former self and feels a pang in the middle of her chest, shifts on the bed, and understands that it was easier to be drunk and outside Bernice than who she has become.

It wasn't until she overheard one of the drunken Whippets refer to someone, her, as "Lisping Buffalo" that she became herself again. After a while, Lola became drunken, belligerent and argumentative. Bernice watched in awe as she tore up and through several friends, acquaintances and strangers.

At one point, Lola began to discuss the efficacy of hygiene and bathing and Bernice was forced to confront another truth: she was being made fun of. She looked down at her raw hands, soft and scarred over from the fire and re-scarred with cuts from the knives at Lola's Little Slice of Heaven, muscled with the vigour with which she pounded Lola's buns and breads.

Farther down at her pale brown legs – revealed and naked in a dirty and torn corduroy miniskirt. Her thin sausage legs encased in too-tight ripped hose. And saw herself as Lola saw her. Ugly. Fat. Dirty. Used. In the summers at home, a fundamentalist minister brought a circus tent to the reserve and preached to the erring population. Screaming "Jesus loves the Red Ones!" to save their souls, he would bellow over the cheap loudspeaker, his incantation echoing for miles. Bouncing off of the water. Lost in the rush of the wind in the trees. Rejected by the stones and arching over hills. And the converts and his invited guests would nod and hum with the intonation just for them, just for the Red Ones. The tent billowed with his conviction and the ground vibrated with the confident resonance of his certitude.

In that moment, the one where she saw her most hated self, it dawned on Bernice that if Jesus does love the Red Ones, he most assuredly would love her. And since he didn't, there must not be a Jesus, either. So Jesus did not weep and Jesus did not save.

She realized she would have to save herself.

She began by throwing her drink at the Whippets, and when this did not have the visual effect she anticipated, she turned the table over, spilling their drinks and purses. The Whippets began writhing, as Whippets do, in their joy at their emotional affrontedness. Their glee in their righteous indignation. Their religious fervour at her saving.

Lola tried to drunkenly hug her, called her honey. And. Something else. Birdgirl. In Cree.

Because Lola spoke to her in kindness she did not punch her.

"Atone." "Vengeance is mine." Bernice whispered in a stunned Lola's leathery ear. She was out of the bar — exit *accompli* before she realized her purse was still under her chair in the barroom. For a brief moment she pondered the vow of poverty but, wobbling on her spiked heels, decided a cab would be in order this evening.

A bit melodramatically she stormed up to the table and grabbed her bag — a nice one, too, she'd lifted it from the Wal-Mart in Grande Prairie — and turned to leave.

"Bernice . . ." Lola looked almost contrite, "I don't think you should go home alone."

"I'm not going home."

"Can I come with you?" Of course, she wanted away from the Whippets.

"Nope."

After that she looked for a cab but ended up teetering on those spikes all the way across town.

She wandered to two other bar/restaurants and looked in the glass doors but did not enter. Whatever she was looking for was not in those places. She walked the blurry blocks home — staying near the water as long as she could and doubling her trip. She sat and stared for the longest time; rose to leave only when she felt light again. She realized, too late, that she had lost her shoes and was instantly bereft. Something passed over, like a cloud, like a storm warning, and she felt heavier and changed.

Lola was waiting in the kitchen when she let herself in the back door. "You okay, honey?"

She had opened her mouth to speak and found that her

tongue could no longer form syllables, the English language became foreign, and although she never could do so with any fluency before, she spoke in her own tongue. Her words, mostly foreign visitors on her tongueterrain, bubbled up like water from a spring.

This time Lola didn't understand. In fact, she looked quite frightened. Bernice let herself be pulled up the stairs and into her suite. The room smelled of old socks and something tomato-ey. Her pile of laundry in the corner near the window almost reached the second pane of glass. It was a temple of sorts; a monument to vanity. She got undressed and put on her baker's uniform: white pants (44), white T-shirt (grey at the neck and armpits) and her nurse's shoes.

"Just lie down, sweetie, you don't need to work today." Lola comforted her, made her sip tea and sat on the floor beside her while she slept.

When she awoke, when she remembered to wake, she realized that she has soiled herself. The stench was comforting and the warmth soothing. The next time she woke up she was dry and didn't notice the smell anymore, although a stain remained.

Her waking time passed slower than her sleeping time, but eventually they blended together for she got no rest. One night she awoke, screaming, with Lola hugging her and patting her, begging her to do something. She couldn't make it out because she no longer speaks that language. She was going under.

"*Hey-ya-hey ay yay yah hah,*" crescendo decrescendo.

She had sunk.

She thinks now about her mother, her soft touch and hurt eyes. Misses her. And something else. The lodge. Where she had gotten her name. Where *Kohkom* had taken them all. Which her mom stopped going to and her father never started going to. The last safe place. She wants to go back, wants that life again, that life before booze, when her uncles, shirtless, had been drummers and shirtless was okay, when she felt the Creator, that the women surrounding her on their side of the lodge were equal, when they all understood themselves to be safe. The first and last safe place.

Her breastbone falls on the place that hurts, her breathing is ragged and pained, and she feels what used to be there. What is supposed to be there. What is no longer there. And. Wants it back. She begins to understand and see that what is piled between her and the last safe place is a succession of bad decisions, only a very few of them hers. She has been in this bed. Since. Then.

Skinny Freda's heels keep click click clicking on the floor of Bernice's room. Bernice can hear her walk across and back the small apartment, her skinny Indian legs tapping a staccato on the faded linoleum. Once in a while, Skinny Freda pauses at the bed as she passes in front of it. Bernice can smell the angst in the room and knows that Freda is considering the situation. Freda is smart. Freda is always considering the situation. Maybe it comes from being the daughter and granddaughter of hunters, or from being a bit of a barroom brawler, but Freda always has a Plan B. Always knows where the exits are. Bernice tries to see the room as she imagines her cousin sees it. She has been – has been what, passed out? Paralyzed? Asleep? Under? She doesn't know. For a long time.

What Bernice also does not know is that Skinny Freda is very close to calling an ambulance. Bernice tries really hard to make herself invisible. And a hospital visit – well that just wouldn't have been good for anyone. She thought, a fleeting thought, that it might have passed through Freda's head that she would get into trouble (from the family, for not shunning her cousin, for endorsing her behaviour, for continuing to love her?) not only for visiting Bernice but also for not reporting her whereabouts. And, as Skinny Freda had proven before, while loyal, she is not blindly so.

She winces when her cousin's clipped, Cree-inflected voice breaks the peace in the room. "Bernice, Bernice, you gotta get up offa your back and join us here in the land," she pauses for effect, "the land of the free. You can't just sit there, lay there with that silly grin on your face. And your pyjamas, come on now."

She scrapes dried food off a pillow.

"Bernice, I am gonna have to call a doctor, you have to eat something. Shit or whatever."

While she seems to be so peaceful, there is something in her body, some laxness or illness that has entered the room, and it has scared the bejeezus out of Freda. Bernice doesn't know what Freda sees, only what she feels. And what she feels is: obligation. To the past. To the *Pimatisewin*. To make one thing right.

Maybe she is bluffing, maybe she is not, Bernice thinks. But calling a doctor, getting any kind of attention, doesn't really pull any fear out of her anymore. As far as she was concerned the worst has happened. If people found her, she would just stay inside of herself.

Freda seats herself at the little desk Bernice pulled from the garbage for a table. She had moved it to the window so she could look out at the street below. "You see Bernice, no matter what happened back home, you gotta deal with the here and now. You got a new life, some friends, a good job."

Freda taps the tobacco into the filter as she lights another cigarette, her old one still burning in an ashtray on the floor. She is not used to being gentle and Bernice knows that the kindness must cost her something. She closes her eyes but imagines Freda inhaling deeply. The smell is too strong in the small space, but still she wants to join Skinny Freda.

She almost flinches and realizes that her cousin was speaking to her from the head of the bed.

"Remember when you and I were kids and we used to take off to Grande Prairie? We used to do our hair for hours and get all dressed up. Do you remember Bernice? Do you?"

Freda stares at Bernice's face and looks for something familiar, something that looks like Bernice.

"You're just a shell now, aren't ya?" she chides her.

"There's no one in there anymore, is there?" Bernice feels panic rise in her as she begins to sense the degree of Freda's fear.

Her cousin's words ring emptily in her ear. "You ain't got nothing to be ashamed of, nothing at all. All that stuff back there, well it's still back there. You come out, Bernice. Freda's

Tracey Lindberg

waiting. And that old lady, she needs you too. Come on Bernice. Come on."

Bernice imagines Skinny Freda in tight white pants, scuffed toeless high heels and a tight black T-shirt. When Skinny Freda is anxious, she touches her face – just like their uncles. She pictures Freda rubbing her temple, absentmindedly scratching her nose. Flicking her ashes, she would pinch her cheeks, Bernice thinks, wondering if she has any colour in her face – what with being inside all of the time.

Freda might have been staring at her puzzle book – she has been marking her vigil with crossword puzzles. She does three a day, between the smoking and talking to Bernice. Bernice thinks that, by now, she probably has a pile as deep as her thumb. It has been weeks since Bernice lay down. Broke down. Went down.

When Bernice and Skinny Freda (she was always Skinny Freda) were kids they used to run to the Loon Lake post office every afternoon to see if anyone had sent them mail. They moved so much that the office was the only place they could be sure they would get mail. They clipped fan mail addresses out of the newspaper and *Tiger Beat* magazine and were sure that Scott Baio, Leif Garrett and Philip McKeon would answer their letters. They also wrote to Pat John care of the CBC. First, they tried writing to him care of Molly's Reach, but the letter was returned. Later, they started sending letters to Pat John/*Beachcombers*, at the CBC. Every time they went to town, maybe once or twice a month, they would drop dozens of letters in the mail for their "Hollywood boyfriends" as *Kohkom* called them. They would write to all of the boys on TV. And in the movies. Each time they sent a batch, Bernice would make sure Jesse got at least one letter from her, no matter who else she wrote to. She reassured him that she liked him best in her letters, told him that she had to write to others since he wasn't writing back, but she understood because he was so busy filming and acting and all. And did he think he would come to Alberta sometime?

At first, no one wrote. After a while, though, pictures and newsletters trickled in. Willie Aames and Anson Williams sent pictures. Bernice let Skinny Freda have those. Jimmy McNichol sent a fan club address and a short photostatted note encouraging them to finish school, no matter what. Freda carried that one to school and showed everyone. Eventually, the prize: Jesse sent a signed picture to "Birdie and Freda." Bernice was overjoyed – she had always loved the name Birdie. She and Skinny Freda shared that picture like a divorced couple share a kid. Bernice opted for weekends and Freda had him all week.

During a fight when they were fifteen, Freda drew a beard and black tooth on the picture. Bernice was so mad she would not speak to her for three weeks. They were never the same after that. Bernice remained nice, but there was something missing in their fun. Like the language they spoke had dialects and they each spoke a different one.

In fact, when she was a teenager, Bernice stopped talking again. After the Christly school and before the Ingelsons', when she was in care. There was no reason to talk then. The group home was so full of sound and so many people spoke for Bernice that she let other voices fill the space. A different silence visited her when she went to the San. Freda never came to see her. It's not like she planned it or that it was expected that she would have visited, and she knows why her cousinsister made herself scarce then. And. When, to a certain degree, Bernice took leave of her body that day of the Christmas pageant Freda stopped seeing her. It was like Bernice's spirit was sleeping, only to awaken on the rarest of occasions.

Bernice got fat, and then fatter and then fatter. She ate with an appetite that she had not earned. She ate like she was not going to eat again. Eventually, her pretty face gave in to the battle she was waging with her fork. Her eyes began to look tiny in her doughy brown face. Her cheeks lost their colour and her hair became lifeless. It was like she had put on the suit of an artist's caricature of Bernice – blown up and expanded. As if the flame of Bernice had consumed her like shrubs eaten by a brush fire.

"Come on, Bernice, keep . . ." Freda wants to say "normal," but Freda probably doesn't really know what that is in this situation. "Going," she announces to the cramped and notably smelly bedroom.

Freda busies herself collecting laundry, emptying ashtrays and tidying up. Bernice hopes her cousin takes in the quiet in the room and not the furious sounds that rise and fall within her. At one point, Bernice hears her thumbing through the posters from the ever-present tube. Bernice vaguely hopes she will not put them up. Those. Are not. That. The afternoon heat hits the storefront and Bernice's living room with a gentle intensity that both women are still unused to. Bernice longs for a cool breeze off the lake like at home. Even on the water here the heat provides a gentle reminder that the B.C. sun can be harsh.

FREDA

The wafting warmth in the apartment serves as a reminder to try to fergodsake get Bernice to the washroom today. Body odour and bile fills the small suite. Not-so-sweet, she thinks with a mean grin. She lights a cigarette to mask the stench, and to busy her hands. Yesterday (was it only yesterday?) she walked to the market to get some cleaning supplies to take care of the mess. While she was out she was certain she saw a glimpse of a former star of Canadian television. His hair was dyed blond and his eyebrows plucked, oh yes quite a dandy indeed, but Freda was almost positive it was the boyman that Bernice had made a fool of herself over her whole life. He was coming out of the magazine shop (News to You) with a copy of *Hustler* magazine.

Figgers, she had thought. *All them Hollywood types are like that.*

Like *that* is precisely why she hadn't told Bernice yet. Not that she'd understand, but there is something in Freda that tells her that Bernice knows *exactly* what's going on in her cruddy little apartment. And certainly, if she does, Freda does not want Bernice to know this about *that*.

"Poor kid, you've had enough of *that* for all of us." She places a compress on Bernice's head, even though she shows no sign of a fever. It calms them both down, though.

When they were kids Bernice was sick a lot. Freda would bring over a bottle of pop, stir the bubbles out and then place wet facecloths on her head while she lay, curled up, on her roll-away cot under the stairs. She always slept under there, never wanted to share a room with Freda. Almost everyone left her alone, seemingly in accordance with her wishes. One door, no window, no escape. *It's amazing that she got – well . . . got out,* Freda thinks.

"Bernice, you will not believe what I bought you." Bernice was the one Cree person on the planet who does not like teasing or being teased. Skinny Freda knows this. Regardless, she continues, "But I will not give it to you until you get up from that damn rat's nest and join me at this little table." She motions to the chair opposite her with her lips.

She holds up a copy of *The Completely Unauthorized Biography (Including Totally Secret Photos) of The Beachcombers.* Bernice lies still. In her shell. In her mess. But Freda has the sense that you get staring at a cat before it springs at you.

"Not coming up for air? Figgers. You always were the most stubborn of the bunch. Remember that time we went to G.P. for groceries? You know, you musta been only fifteen at the time."

Skinny Freda wants to sit on the side of the bed, but she won't do that because somewhere inside of her she knows Bernice would not want that. She thinks better of it, and Bernice feels her hovering near the bed.

"Ah Bernice, come back. Come back to me. Come back just to show us how we couldn't wreck you." She does not notice the flinch in Bernice's right hand, and Freda puts her head on her arms and sleeps, sitting up, for the fourth day in a row.

LOLA

Lola sits and stares at the mess that is/was Bernice and wonders what the hell to do.

"Christ, I am too old for this," she says. But, she doesn't believe that.

Rather than wonder about what melted down in that kid, she thinks about how to get her out of bed. That was one big buffalo of a gal. Come to think of it, she is more a calf now than a cow. She washes her face, cleans Bernice like a bad housekeeper would – surfaces only. Lola also continues to bring Bernice comfort food, enough for two weeks. What she cannot observe is what happens in her absence. While she was gone, Bernice had, well she couldn't be sure she had eaten it, but she had disappeared it. None of it was cooked or heated and The Kid seems not to have eaten anything in days.

And does she ever shit? Lola has been listening for the toilet, watching to see if Bernice changes her position in bed, leaves a drop of ice cream on a sheet, creaks a floorboard overhead. Nothing. Like she's some sort of. Ghost.

As her employee/tenant stares blankly at the ceiling, Lola wonders what the fuck she did to deserve this.

Their days have taken on an amorphous feeling. Light becomes sleep time, dark is when Bernice's almost imperceptible shaking starts. Sleep is preferable. Lola considers stopping visiting, but instead comes and sits with Bernice when the other women seem to need a break. She does, however, leave the food just outside the door. *If she is faking it, she should at least have to walk for it,* she reasons.

Tracey Lindberg

She looks at the thinner, much thinner face of The Kid and pronounces, "You gotta get outta here, kiddo." Upon reflection, she adds, "Although you have more colour than the rest of us."

FREDA

Freda opens her purse and takes out the crumpled lists she has been snatching whenever she sees them. Several are Bernice's. There is also one from each of the other occupants of the bakery. All sit on top of the journal that Bernice has been writing ingredients in for years. She thumbs through it, stops at the first entry and wonders how the hell she is going to find bison marrow in Vancouver. And. Puts her foot on the gas. And. Goes hunting.

VAL

Valene is trying to be humble. For her, it is much like speaking a foreign language. You don't get to be the gorgeous big woman in the room (she checks herself, forming her tongue around the new word: "Biggest") without a heaping helping of confidence or madeconfidence. She figures she has been faking it since she was making it for so long . . . maybe she can do that with humility, too.

"I ain't gonna get no lessons in that around here." She points with her lips in the direction of Lola's, carrying on an imaginary conversation with herself.

Lola and Freda have been filling the quiet in the bakery with nonsensical and non-stop chatter about themselves, and it was getting under Val's skin. Their words tumbled over each other like puppies some days, each waiting to tell the other of their adventures, favourite something or other, or something else that Val did not understand. There. Was also something else in the room. Val knew it and could feel it, but she didn't know if those two could yet.

"Not like sense is suddenly gonna stop in for dinner with 'em." She smiles a little smile. And then remembers. Humility. Chuffs at herself. Rolls her eyes. The two little seniors on the grass with her give her a wide berth as she walks by.

In any event, she is glad that Freda has gone to the city, gives them all a bit of a change.

She heaves herself up onto the top of a picnic table, can't feel her skirt and hopes that it has stayed down. That's all she needs – to be the crazy lady who talks to herself and flashes people near the spirit tree.

Humble, humble, humble. Maybe if she just thinks the word over and over, then she will get there.

Cigarette, cigarette, cigarette.

She has a pack with her and knew she would smoke, but has not had any since she was a teenager. Nope, bannock and butter were her drugs of choice. So, it does not sit well with her that she has such a craving right now.

She and her sister used to sneak smokes from *Kohkom* and sneak out to go puff by the water. The craving that has taken her now was familiar then. Two? Three times a day, she and Maggie would sneak past the old lady and sit by the water, talking about boys and life outside of Loon.

She has a longing for Maggie's quiet company so fierce that her eyes prick with tears. They were spirit sisters, one bigger than the other, but reflective surfaces of the beauty that ran in their family. When Maggie was in her teens, she had the most gorgeous hair – black as night, thick and long. Val envied that hair.

Humble, humble, humble.

She also had cheekbones. Fantastic, arching and sharp bones that were at once bird-like and reminiscent of some other time. Some other people. No slouch herself, Val remembers, her own big, beautiful Cree nose and finer and curlier hair. Oh, but men loved to look at the Meetoos sisters. Valene was the talker but Maggie had a rich silence about her that people wanted to reside in. She had, Valene realizes for the first time, a real peace with solitude unlike anything she would ever know. Her sister first lived in silence. Then. In noise.

Her breast hurts. She does not have to remind herself to be humble. She has come to offer prayers to the tree. Not for the tree, like many many other of her and many peoples have done. To the tree. She wants to ask the pitiful thing (really, she isn't sure if it is still alive) to help her family. What's left of her family But. The one thing she really feels, sitting here, smoking and crying (and, to be frank, farting a bit), is thankfulness to Maggie. For Maggie. About Maggie. She can't do the emotional math yet, but she knows she has two daughters because Maggie gave them to her. She is overcome with humility and quiet certitude. She has to raise her girls right. Birdie and Freda. Her girls.

She takes her tobacco offering to the tree and asks for help. Without shame. Without fear.

"I am pitiful," she prays and cries.

"Please help me," she cries and prays.

One thing. She can smell moosehide and Tabu perfume. Maggie.

⚬⚬⚬

Bernice looks at Lola without opening her eyes and sees Lola's mouth moving, but can no longer hear her. Bernice has heard her in the shop below at times, but doesn't know what anyone is saying to the customers and friends who visit. She only knows it is low tone this and murmured voice that. She can no longer make out words, she supposes. She can hear, though.

> *Hey-ya–hey ay yay yah hah.*
> *Hey-ya–hey-ay-yay-yah-hah.*
> *Hey ay yay hey yah*
> *Hey ay yay hah.*

Lola shakes her head, turns on the TV and leaves.

Bernice feels the familiar vibration of the opening strain of the *Frugal Gourmet* theme song. In her waking hours she knows that this is a vision within a vision, and that it has some meaning for her. She is not certain she could ever bring herself to mention the cooking show to an Elder in order to get guidance.

"*Keskawayatis.*"*

---

* "She is behaving foolishly."

acimowin

"What's a young owl like you doing out here all on your own?"
the third leering truck driver
Who
happens to be a trickster asks.
"My mom got sick in Victoria, she sent me money to come and
see her,
but I wanted to get her something nice so I decided to catch some
rides along the way,"
she says in an
easy caw.
"I wouldn't have worried, but she came out here to bring my sister
home,
and she lives on the . . ."
tearing up
for effect
and to rule
out further conversation,
she seems to muster her strength,
"streets."
The wolf
nods sullenly and clucks sympathetically,
which she thinks is nice
until
she notices
he has his thing in his hand.

12

LOVE THE ONE THAT BRUNG YOU

Mîcimâpôhkêw: s/he makes stew, s/he makes broth

pawatamowin

She raised her eyes in the lodge and tried to see who was there.

There was no one she recognized — everyone seemed quite old.

She heard a murmur from beside her and reached for the pipe.

With the greatest of effort, she raised her head and saw that the Frugal Gourmet was offering her the pipe.

She walked from the sweatlodge, across the meadow, to her home. The steam rose into the air off of her wet clothes and hung above her in a dense and sluggish fog as she lifted unwieldy left leg and then unwieldy right. The Pimatisewin *is right beside her house.*

There was a piece of paper taped to the tree. In her dreamwalk, she was graceful and light. As she moved closer to the tree, she noticed two things that scared the crap out of her.

The piece of paper had the words "basil and corn flour" *written on it.*

Also, it was in her handwriting.

S KINNY FREDA HAS BEEN GONE, maybe two days, Bernice doesn't really know how long. After a while she had heard her and Lola talking downstairs. She considers getting up to crouch next to the heating grate to eavesdrop, but is conserving her strength. And. There was nothing interesting enough in their tone to get her out of bed. Physically, she doesn't know if she *can* get up. She is aware, somewhere in her body, that things are shutting down. But from the same place, Bernice knows this is okay. She has not resigned herself to anything but occupying the space she is in, taking one raspy breath whenever she can, and trying to come back to her skinself. When she does this, she has peace with whatever happens. A knowledge is born in her: that she has been to Then. And. She might not make it back. To Now.

Little pieces of Now trickle in to her. One time Bernice heard Lola and Freda talking about Chuck Woolery from the *Love Connection* and the next day, well she thought it was the next day, the bakery didn't open. She thinks that maybe they went visiting or something but wasn't sure. She had felt a little peevish that they had gone without saying anything to her, but also that she had better keep her mouth shut.

Skinny Freda may be a lot of things, Bernice thinks, but she is no fool and she does not suffer fools. When she does wake up, if she wakes up, Bernice thinks, she'd better have a pretty damn good story to tell her. One thing Freda likes more than cigarettes and honky-tonk music is a good story. She doesn't quite know what she will tell Freda if she unsinks. She can feel her body now, it's loose and stiff at the same time. Her head, though, that will be the hard part. Part of her was lost for so long that it is hard to enunciate what, exactly, she has found. That she left for the first time the night of the pageant. That she steeled herself at the Christly school, and found in that steel a chance of escape. That care, the group home, lent her the knowledge that she could be strong in silence. That the Ingelsons taught her that home was not a mélange of stuff, kindness and chance. That Edmonton, her real school, taught her to change, because she had to. That returning to Loon taught her what family was not. Too much, too few words to describe it and none of them adequate to explain it. Nope, Freda would not like this story, she supposes.

Bernice suspects that Skinny Freda is up to something. She's started buying smokes (not rolling her own) and has worn lipstick for two days. Bernice wonders if someone is coming. Maybe Freda told someone, she thought. Maybe she called Momma. Bernice would like to but finds herself unable to shake her head. She knows what no one is telling her. Momma is gone. She had pretended she believed it before, to punish herself. Now, she can feel Maggie's absence, like the smell of smoke once cedar has burned. She is gone, Bernice tells herself, but even in her sleepingwake state, she can feel her mom. Not around her or near, but in another way that she can't quite figure out.

One thing she is certain of, and that is that Skinny Freda – the same Skinny Freda who swore off white men because they "smelled funny" – and Lola are planning something. They keep laughing and talking and Bernice wonders, a bit grumpily truth be told, what they are doing when they are not spending their time taking care of her. She would like to chew her nails and is too weak to do so; she tries to look at them and sees through some haze (is that new? Now? Then?) that there is silver paint and sparkles on them. That Freda, she thought that if your toes and fingers looked good, you would have to feel good because they're closest to the world. Bernice almost smiles.

That crazy Skinny Freda.

acimowin

When she looks back, that old young owl,
She sees that
her home, her tree, had become
ravaged with wolf urine
and twisted with heat.
Curled and gnarled, she is unable to sleep there.
She begins to travel at nights
because she cannot sleep in her home.
She doesn't know what
She's lookin' for
But she keeps goin' and goin'.

Tracey Lindberg

13

HOME COMING/COMING HOME

Kiwehtahiwew: s/he takes people home with him/her

pawatamowin

She stood beside the sweat and bent at the waist. The entryway, much like the scenery in Hollywood movie sets, was made to appear small from a distance. As she drew nearer to it she saw that the entrance was not becoming proportionally wider. The door stayed the same size, even though the lodge itself grew larger as she approached.

As she drew closer to the hole, she instinctively knew (as she knows when she sees a dress too small for her on a perfectly sized mannequin) that she would not fit in the entry.

She didn't want to but knows that she must attempt to enter. She squeezed herself in to the depth of her armpits, the ring of the doorway cutting into her like a too-tight casing on a sausage.

Womanly hands grab her, smooth her belly with lambda olive oil and she is pulled into the lodge like a reverse birth.

S HE IS DYING, THEY THINK. None of the three says anything about it, there is no reluctant or covert admission. Last night Val had lain in the same bed as her niece and whispered to her all night. Then she sang to the light she saw passing from her un/natural daughter. She had warbled lullabies, sweet walking songs, and finally "Blood is Thicker than Water" by Andy Gibb. Through it all, Bernice lay motionless (no one says "lifeless" but everyone thinks it) beside her, wrapped in blankets. This morning, when Freda came up to check on them, words passed between Val and herself in one look. She had walked down the stairs, quietly in her baker's shoes, picked up the phone and started dialing. That should have been a harder decision, but Freda just called everyone in the family and left it to them to make their own minds up about coming.

When she was done, she walked to Lola and they hugged, little fierce trees, withstanding the wind.

Val sits beside her niece, on the floor, staring at her for most of the morning. Love falls like thistle seeds and lands gently on top of, around, near, beside Bernice. If she is aware of Val, her love, the seedlings or her dire circumstance, she gives no indication.

Late last night, when Val had told her, "It's okay, Birdie, you do what you have to do; you go where you have to go," Bernice did just that.

And. What she had to do was find the space where her memory could live peaceably with her body. She could not take her body with her, so she willed herself to leave.

She found herself freed, in a way she had never been when

Tracey Lindberg

she did the change on the streets of Edmonton. Light, in a way she had never felt when she left her body in the room under the stairs. She finds herself, this morning, unconfined by the agitation and nervousness that she always has. She had no coyote's wariness. Found that she does not possess the cunning of a wolf. In truth, she feels rather like a bird. Her body below her shines with some invisible and barely perceptible light. Her auntie kneels beside her, praying like a nun. Bernice sees versions of younger Val, wilder Val, crazier Val. And feels such love for them all.

Taking care to hold her feelings with her, she inhales sharply and flies. She doesn't know if it is through the window, through place or through time. But she is able.

She flies home. To the place where she learned to love and the place where she learned fear. Home. Where her youth mixed with her experience in a strange alchemy, leaving her self split like oil and vinegar.

⁓

Lola cannot stop moving. If she does, she is afraid she will run upstairs again to see The Kid. And she can't do that. That big girl, formerly big girl, fermenting like an ale in her attic and no one is going to do a thing about it. God help her if she gets into trouble with them two around.

She looks at a clearly distressed Freda and is flooded with emotion. Some she understands. Some she does not. That little brown woman looks like she is carrying the weight of the world on her shoulders. And the aunt? Good lord, the aunt is all "She will do what she has to" this and "Let's just wait awhile" that. Lola wants to throttle her today.

The Kid herself looks . . . well, it is hard to put it into words. Certainly there is some sort of . . . "Melting." Lola says her thought out loud.

"What?" Freda looks up sharply.

"Nothing, hon, you go about yer business," Lola says gently.

Yes, The Kid looks like she is melting. Dimming. Half gone. But. There is something else, too. Goddamn her for thinking it, but The Kid looks gorgeous. Pale, sickly, too skinny and certainly anything but robust. But. She also looks lovely. *Like her body fits her spirit*, Lola thinks and then chases that thought away.

She pulls out the boxes of food that the three of them had been bringing home each week, intending to throw them out – Lola has never had the resolve that Freda has or the faith of Val. Those boxes sit in her kitchen, frustrating her with their uselessness. Instead of trashing them, she reads the lid of the first box:

Wattleseed
Masala powder
chiba (wormwood leaf)
Dried cloudberry
Caraway
Aniseed
Chrysanthemum pollen
bitter orange
Angelica root

Tracey Lindberg

lemon
myrtle sprinkle
bergamot leaves
Epazote leaves
lavender
Jalap root
Tasmanian pepper berries
Cheezies

Skinny Freda had driven Lola's car to Vancouver to get most of it. Lola and Valene had gathered the rest from the land or had sent for it from Little Loon. In the walk-in freezer there is another box with wild game, gut, bones, noses. *Everything but the kitchen sink*, she thinksnipes.

What on earth had they been thinking? Lola wonders. All of this stuff, just sitting here going to waste. She goes to throw it out at the curb. After sitting and having a smoke, she thinks better of it and goes to fetch it back. When she reaches the door, Freda meets her there and grabs the door from her, marching into the room with another box piled high in her brown arms.

She is crying when Lola takes the box from her. "There, there, sugar. It's okay. Let's just make some work to keep our hands busy, eh?" the old woman says, grabbing some stationery and starting to label the exotic contents of the box.

꩜

Freda goes out for a smoke behind the bakery. And. Weeps like she has lost her best friend.

Valene is growing impatient with Lola and Freda. They are acting like two teenagers who are in the blush of first love. They think that Val can't see how they look at each other. Smitten. Lusty. It has been all she could do to pry them apart to get them to listen to her. After hearing Bernice's sleep-talking about *Pimatisewin*, she sat the two women down to talk about the tree and its illness, not really sure why she was doing it. She sensed it was important, though, and told them a story about the tree of life and how some crazy Sechelt woman thinks she has found one of the four about an hour from Gibsons.

"Are you trying to tell me that The Kid is here because she heard a tree call her?" Lola had cackled.

Pressing her nails into Lola's knee, Skinny Freda said, "Stranger things have happened. Birdie is tapped into something, always has been. May as well be the tree."

So, they now sit in the kitchen, all of their heads pregnant with thoughts too big to speak – each of them fearful the grandness of the lexicon would choke them if they should utter a word.

There is a knock at the door. The relatives are arriving.

acimowin

At the top
of her lungs,
the owl hoots hoots hoots
as he soars over a shiny spot on the ground below her.
Circling the shine, her black eyes reflect the shine flickering off
what she thinks, at first, is a very small pool of water.
Beneath the owl,
the sun on the bald man's head
reflects
and dances as he walks
towards a very small and crooked tree.

14

CEREMONY – WHAT SHE MUST DO

iskwew: woman

pawatamowin

She has left the lodge, crossed through the tall grass, steam lifting to the night air.

She goes home to her room, and looks — surprised — to find that the TV has been placed on the desk. The screen shines blue from the glow of the bad reception.

There are scenes from old Westerns, Chief Dan George, Jay Silverheels and Burt Reynolds flicker against the wall. Finally the Frugal Gourmet (well, it looks like him but he's wearing a white hat) comes on. She looks at the television intently and realizes he is cooking in her mom's kitchen.

She wanders down the stairs and into the coolness of Lola's kitchen, the tiles feel soft and giving. She opens the swinging door between the living room and the kitchen. And sees him. There.

He has pots and pans scattered about him where he sits on the floor. He is drumming, she recognizes the song as an old women's song, and as he begins to drum she reads his soiled recipe card.

1 pinch tarragon

2 cups baby bok choy

2 tsp. Chilean red bean (dried)

1 pinch sifted bean meal

3 cups kangaroo tallow

I N HER ROOM, Bernice's eyes open.

Bernice sits up, no longer a bird and claiming her human form. Writes the ingredients down on the list she has pulled from the roll of loose flesh on her belly, and rises shakily to her feet.

And realizes. She is on her time.

15

THE SHIFT – WHO SHE HAS BECOME

otâcimow: a Storyteller, one who tells legends

pawatamowin
In her dreams, and there were four days' worth of dreams, she
is an owl.
Flying over
The Tree of Life.
She keeps carrying
twigs and leaves
to the Tree
in order
to nest there.

She carries berries and food to her nest and knows she is
Feeding herself from the Tree.
Feeding her life to the Tree.

In another dream, she is afraid
to ask Pimatisewin
to kill the wolves.

She knows it will not, but still wants to ask it.
"Not all wolves are bad," she hears.
The sick wolves leave the pack, *she knows.*

On the fourth day of her moons,
on the fourth day of feeding the Tree,
on the fourth day of dreaming
she dreams of feasts
feasts and feasts and feasts

She dreams of going home
She dreams that she is loved.

"ICAN'T BELIEVE WE ARE DOING THIS," Skinny Freda grunts as she takes an armload of pine boughs from Valene off the back of the rented Ram.

Valene had the boughs sent from Kelly Lake, even though she didn't know why. *For this*, she thinks and gingerly carries them to the *Pimatisewin*. She ignored Lola's questions. She never thought she'd say it, but that woman thinks too much.

"You know, in the old days they used to do this all the time." She stops to breathe. After a minute or two, she resumes. "Old ladies would take the young ones when we had our first moons and put us in a lodge built for it."

"But it was the first moons," Skinny Freda starts to argue, then stops when she sees Valene's face.

"They'd lay down them boughs and we would lay there away from everyone." Val smiles. "Seems to me I went there at twelve."

"I know, I understand the whole strong medicine thing, but don't you think it's weird for her to be doing this . . ." Skinny Freda chooses carefully and then says, "Now? She's too sick to lay there for four days." She nods over her shoulder at Bernice, who stares straight ahead and who is too weak to lift the boughs, even the little ones.

Valene does not comment and helps her not-so-big-any-more niece from the truck and leads her to the shelter they had built beside the *Pimatisewin*. "Now you just lay there and make good medicine, my girl." She hugs her and goes back to wait in the truck. She sits there four days. Lola and Freda try to stagger her off, but it's her girl and she will hear none of it. She checks on Bernice occasionally and hears her singing. Hears her crying. Hears her praying. On the fourth day, she walks to her daughter, takes her hand, prepares her tea, and takes her home to the bakery to cook.

❧

A few hours ago, they were all sitting in the kitchen when Bernice appeared, like a vision, in the doorway at the foot of the stairs. Wearing a skirt, the shawl Valene had made and her new purple T-shirt, she had a box in her hands and the women saw that she had a collection of food, spices, roots and leaves that rivalled the ones they have on the table.

"I need to cook," she had croaked.

Valene pursed her sizable lips. "Just rest a minute, Birdie, we have time."

"No, let's go," Bernice said with a firmness that no one knew lived within Bernice.

With that, the four women headed to the kitchen, where they have been for hours. Every so often, Bernice walks slowly past the front room of the bakery, which is filled beyond full with relatives and strangers who have gathered for what they thought was a funeral. And a wake. Bernice has so little energy that she merely managed to greet everyone with a smile before she returned to the kitchen. Several female relatives jumped up to help.

"No," Bernice had croaked. "Just them." She pointed with her lips to the bedraggled family she had formed in Gibsons. "Just us four."

Tracey Lindberg

That womenfamily, Lola, Val and Skinny Freda, had followed her into the kitchen. They spoke in hushed tones, like
they were in a library, and every so often she could hear the
plump fullness of Valene's words and the hard nut of Lola's
as they talk while working in the kitchen. She had given the
three women her ingredient list, those ingredients that came
to her in her dreamstate, those that had come to them as gifts,
and they had set about organizing the kitchen. Intent for
hours, she can barely make out their feasttalk. The words are
frothy and full. Unintelligible and edible.

"Wasting fasting faking lasting baking."

Bernice remembers something. "We can only speak kindly
while preparing this food." She shot Lola and Freda indepen-
dent glances. "And you two, stop mooning over each other and
get busy, please."

She is glad when Skinny Freda offers to help read the ingredients and Bernice even lets her and Val carry out the pots and
pans from the pantry to the kitchen. They are too big for her to
lift. Her arms rattle with the effort of lifting, they had cramped
when she mixed, gone numb as she diced. She gives instructions to her madefamily and the four of them set about making
the feast that Bernice has been dreaming about her whole life.

They mix and measure. Sift and sieve.

Whip and pour. Stir and simmer. Chop and dice. Bernice
is careful not to touch the pots and pans or even the cutlery
with her bare hands. She woke up pained to realize that she
seemed to be hypersensitive to touch, smell and sound. Her
heightened awareness balks at the sensory feast. She is afraid
to find out if this acute bodily response extends to taste.

She lines up the ingredients alphabetically because her vision is cloudy and precision required. At the *R*s she realizes that she has forgotten ratroot. As she pulls the ingredients around her, she recognizes the clanking of dishes and muffled tones as her family sets the table in expectation of the feast. Time seems to run out and she hardly knows it is finished until the haze lifted off her vision and she realizes the dishes are done and the remainder of the ingredients put away.

She carefully tucks the medicines in the cupboard and, after a second thought, stores the foods Skinny Freda had brought from the city and those that Val and Lola had bought and gathered and sets them next to her medicines on the shelf. Medicines. *Maskihky.*

She wonders when they will ever use creamed horseradish and minced ginger.

Once done, she puts the offering together, gets the old pine cradleboard and fastens some of the pots and pans to it carefully and with steady fingers – steadier than they have been in a long time. The smells and the textures of the food no longer delight her, and while she does not feel nauseous, she is still unsure about her reaction to the feast. Mint mingled with moose, acorn with pistachio. *Maskihky* with pâté.

Valene tells the family, friends and strangers who have come in anticipation of the *event* waiting in the restaurant dining room to meet them at the *Pimatisewin*. The hushed room had watched as Bernice fastened the bundle and carried the cradleboard out the door and down the front steps.

"Let's take the Ram, it'll be faster," Lola says, walking past her ancient Malibu.

They load the cradleboard and Bernice into the back and journey through the night to the *Pimatisewin,* a convoy of would-be mourners and now celebrants.

During the trip, her body aches, but Bernice refuses to sleep, listening to her family talk in the background. She knows now that *Pimatisewin* had been waiting for her. For all of them: Valene, Skinny Freda and Lola, the people who came from home, the people her friend Lettie and her old man brought from Sechelt. It was waiting to be fed, to have nations unite in one place.

The colours of the night sky stripe and smudge across the windowpane of the cab and out of her vision. It is not a full moon, but it was a clear evening.

Bernice's stomach rumbles pleasantly.

When they get to the tree, several people have already arrived and set up smudges and a fire. They are gathered in a circle around it.

The four women gingerly unpack the feast offering, and place it at the base of the tree, giving the earth thanks for all that they have, for the clarity to be able to see it and for having been given the gift to survive. Taking care not to spill anything they feed their relative. The earth around *Pimatisewin* soaks up the exotic and the sacred, taking the food to its roots, its branches and its bark.

Having left Bernice at the tree to make her offering, Valene and Freda seem not to be able to speak her name.

They sit in silence, smoke filling the cab.

"She gonna be okay, Auntie?" Skinny Freda doesn't know about comfortable silence, Valene thinks.

She purses her ample lips. Thinks about it for a few minutes. "She'll be better off, no matter what." Thinks better of it when she sees Freda's fists fearfully clenched and adds with sureness, "She'd better be. She's got a kitchen to run and people to feed when she's done here."

Tracey Lindberg

acimowin

That owl?
She changed herself.
And she become little enough to fly
Faster and higher than any birds
In the bush
She take with her the crow, the raven and the eagle.
They fly in a line all the way to
The special tree.
They had to take care of that
Special tree
You know.
All four of them had to fly up!
Up! Up! Up!
And closer
And closer
to the special tree.

On the ground before her, the food they have made for *Pima-tisewin* has leeched into the soil and has disappeared. She feels some energy in her limbs, as if she has eaten the food herself, and stands up, the Cree on her tongue having flowed to the tree. Without a word, Valene, Lola and Freda return and take their places beside her, help her up and walk her to the truck.

"We gotta feast to go back to," she croaks to the wimmin.

"Yup," Lola says. "You gotta house full of friends and relatives waiting to be fed." She says it almost giddily; she didn't know how much she loved having people around until they came. She doesn't quite understand the offering, and the feast even less, but Lola sparkles with richness from being a part of it all.

Freda helps Bernice up into the back of the cab and then gets in the front door to sit by Lola. Valene pops in the back row of the cab, careful to bring the cradleboard with her. The sun, just coming up, lights their way.

"That tree looks bigger already!" Lola says, gazing out the back window as they drive away.

"How you feeling?" Val says to her niece, concerned about the days before the four-day fast and what it cost Bernice to come out of that.

"I am feeling like I have a story to tell you," Bernice says.

acimowin

One time there was an owl
And that owl, you know what she did?
She flew home and decided to
Clean up her house.
She took all of the medicines she could hold
In her beak, gathered all of her bird friends and family
And told them she was going to make
A ceremony.
When the wolves come,
She scared 'em away with owl medicine.
She decided to ask
for a special thing — she wanted
The wolves to go away.
But, the wolf was a trickman
And instead of taking the life in the wolves
He put new life in her.
So, yeah, the owl was happy too.
That's the thing about the owl,
She's not like udder birds.
That one, she will sit there
And eyes open or closed
You know that one knows you are there.
They say she don't sleep,
But we know better.
She always looking out for animals —
Don't mess with her house.

Epilogue

ati-itohtew: s/he begins going along

pawatamowin

*Maggie sees herself: young and pretty. She is holding Bernice's
hand and helping her through the muskeg. They sit on some moss
and dry their feet and legs; Kohkom talks to them in Cree and the
young girl listens raptly. Valene comes up into the muskeg, and she
knows it's a dream now, because Birdie's hands are brown and
bear no trace of the ravages of the fire.*

*She smells them before she sees them. They smell like your sharp-
est fear. Heads down, shoulders hunched, they smell women and are
excited – almost unable to contain their gait. She holds Bernice to
her and makes a grab for Freda but is quite unable to hold them.
They are gelatin and she keeps grabbing them but can't keep a grip.*

*Valene takes them and puts them under her belly flap. Kohkom
is still as can be. Maggie feels something in her bones. Lets go of
her girl. And walks towards the wolves.*

MAGGIE

S HE WAS SITTING on a bus. In the window, she saw the pain etched deep into her face. And. Something else. Her reflection showed her a *mososkwew.** Someone with no love. No children. That ache that used to occupy the gash of removal was now more like a bruise. It only hurt when she touched it. So. She didn't.

Maggie hopped off the bus and started walking down the street. She had looked at the little map of Vancouver that she grabbed from a coffeehouse in Gibsons. They had terrible tea, but she hadn't had a good one since she left home. Days ago. Days in strange cars with strange travellers to get to a place she knew nothing about. Gibsons had been a nice surprise, though. The place was bigger than she had imagined, with the same trees and coastline that she saw on the TV. But, no flat picture could do justice to the feeling of the land. She hadn't travelled much but had been enough places to know that this was not always the case. She felt something move in her when she was on that land. Something powerful, joyous and horrific at the same time.

She had gone to see the tree everyone was talking about. Something in her would not rest until she saw it. When she got there, a few people were around, but no one was camped out there on a death watch. Back home, people had said there were crowds out at the tree near Gibsons, but if there was one it was long gone by the time Maggie got there. She was the only person there for portions of the day. She went and sat near the tree, on the ground, trying to see if it was alive. To her

* Spinster.

eye, it looked like it was dead. There was a smell of something though. It took her a minute to recognize it: it smelled like dirt. Not garden dirt. Not forest dirt. But white dirt, like in the old stories. When she was alone, she talked to it. It was a relative, anyways, so she thought it was only right. She started out cordially and ate lunch with the tree, offering it tobacco and then some of her coffee and muffin.

Later in the afternoon, she had to wait for a skinny little woman in an old car (Malibu?) to leave. She kept sitting in her car and, to Maggie, it felt like she was waiting for her to leave. Maggie walked a bit and went to sit down on a picnic bench, had a smoke and then walked back to the little tree. That little white woman was still in her car, still staring at the tree. Maggie walked over to it and took her seat on the grass again.

Once it got dark and they ran out of small talk, Maggie told the tree her secrets. About her brothers. About growing up and away from them. About her kids. About Bernice and how she was in the San. About the *Pimatisewin* in her family's territory. About the fundraisers to make it better.

Before she left — she had to catch the 10:20 bus to Vancouver — she pulled out a little pouch and said a prayer to the tree. She dug a hole near its base and planted her thanks and good wishes in the earth. Walking to the bus depot, a feeling landed in her. Something familiar but old. Like she hasn't felt it in a while. She wondered if it's just her head playing tricks on her because she has been behaving since she left home.

She walked to the tiny bus depot, just making it in time. The trip takes two hours. This seems crazy to Maggie, since the little map says it is only a pinkie-nail away. A pinkie-nail is about fifty miles. It didn't matter. She was in no rush.

Walking from the bus depot, she had to ask people for directions three or four times. Some just walk away from her. One man asks her to be more specific.

"Where on the Eastside?" He had looked at her, concerned. "You know, you shouldn't go there at this time. You could get . . ."

"Missing." Maggie smiles at him kindly. "I will be fine, thank you. Can you tell me where the bars are?"

At that, presuming whatever he presumes about Indian women going to Eastside bars, he gave her directions.

She had never been to Vancouver. Never been to a city this big. Never been to the Indian bars in any city. She thought about her family, sends a prayer to Valene and Bernice. She chose this city and this neighbourhood because she knows someone like her can disappear here.

She finds the bar. Heard the music.

Hey-ya-hey ay yay yah hah.

Hey-ya-hey-ay-yay-yah-hah.

Hey ay yay hey yah

Hey ay yay hah.

Walked in the door. And did.

Acknowledgements

I would like to thank, sincerely, my mom, Gloria Belcourt, my aunties (and little mothers) Donna, Val and Bunny, and my sister Cindy for teaching me about good women. Bernice gets better because they are good and treated me like a healthy, smart, writing daughter, niece and sister before I knew I was any of those things. Maria Campbell has taught, mentored and bossed me around since the day we met. This work would not exist without her critical eye. She was the first to read it and the last to read it. My stepmother Sally made a home for five strangers and provided us with home and shelter. I am thankful to her every day.

This has been an incredibly hard book to write. I am able to do so because my dad, Warren Lindberg, the late and great Harold Cardinal and the still great Chief Bernard Ominayak taught me about good men and how good men listen to women. Each has, at different times, offered me home and safety. I am richer for knowing them. I am thankful as well to Elder Stan Wilson who checked my Cree and who saw this work as part of a spectrum of freeing writing. My brothers Korey and Kris are raising good men, and I am thankful for the love they put into the world.

My agent, Carolyn Swayze, took this ragged manuscript and got it on the desk of the lovely Jennifer Lambert at HarperCollins. Jennifer has made this something readable and absorbable and I am thankful to her for that. She brought in Jane Warren for some of the heavy lifting and she made the book better.

I am thankful to the people and the inherent leadership of the Lubicon Lake Nation who endure, survive and thrive. Thanks particularly to Chief Ominayak and The Elders Council, Councillors and the Whitehead family, who have provided me with a place to sleep, belly laughs over meals and a lifetime of lessons. I am also thankful to the people of my ancestral home, the Kelly Lake Cree Nation, for providing me with a safe place to land.

Priscilla Campeau, Leah Schwerin, Carol Gale – all book lovers and true loves of mine – fed me, my brain and my soul. They are the reflection within which I can best see myself.

For many, many reasons, I am thankful to my friend and love Duncan Cook. For teaching me about healthy men, strong mothers and kind daughters – all under one roof.

The Phils in my life let me talk and write to them my ideas and snippets of drafting. Thank you to my good friends Jeffrey Keller and Darren Dugan. My friend Bevan Audstone taught me about openness and boundaries.

Kate Sutherland, Larissa Behrendt, Constance Backhouse and Martha Minow told me that I could write and should write. They read my stuff along the way and encouraged me to write in my own way, own time and own voice. I am forever thankful for them. They, along with my sisters Bev Jacobs, Val Napoleon, Candice Metallic, and Janice Makokis, Ivy Lalonde and Tanya Kappo took it as a given that I was smart and kind. In turn, I came to believe it.

I am thankful to Elder Stanley Wilson for sharing his thoughts with me on the use of my mothertongue in this book. As well, I am grateful to the Cree Language Resource Project (CLRP) dictionary and the Online Cree Dictionary for much of the Cree language and many of the translations in this work.

Finally, for any mistakes I have made in my writing, my interpretation, my thoughts, I am sorry. This book is meant to free, not to capture, a life. For those who see themselves in Bernice, I hope this frees you a little, too.

FOR BOOK CLUBS:
An Author Interview

Who is Bernice?

Bernice Meetoos is a big Halfbreed (Cree) woman. She is from Kelly Lake, but has no reserve. She lives at Loon Lake, Alberta. Her family has a house on the reserve but they are not status Indians and are not allowed to live there. She is smart, gentle and damaged by a childhood that blew up and splattered everyone around her. She is an adventurer and a bookworm. She is beautiful.

Where is Loon Lake?

The fictional Loon Lake is a reserve in what is now known to many as Alberta. If it existed, it would be north of Grande Prairie and east of Dawson. It has forest all around and a few big hills. Grande Cache with a different splendour and less incline.

Why is there so little about Maggie in the book?

Maggie is the fifth woman in the book. I wanted her to be present and a driving force, but I didn't want her to overshadow Bernice. The mother's story and essence can overshadow and be more intense than the child's, sometimes. For Bernice to truly *be* the story, she had to be, in an emotional sense, alone.

Also, I didn't want to indict Maggie. The pain that visits Bernice is no one's fault, but also, no one takes responsibility in the text. I wanted the reader to know that Maggie has life, spirit and kindness, and that she has a sense of ownership of the problems facing her family. I did not want to detail them because Bernice would not know them and I didn't want to hyper-responsibilitize the women in the work.

There is a book in Maggie. I don't think you have heard the last of her.

Why the shifting verb tense?

Bernice is able, eventually physically but at the outset mentally, to shift time and space. She is able to move about her life with fluidity and no timeline. The emotions, the events or the healing may move her and define where and who she is. I didn't want the verbs to control her, but to serve as an indicator of her fluency with time.

What do the stories of these women represent?

I think they can represent the multiplicity of women's experience. There certainly is a sense that women can make their own families, and that diverse women can have entirely separate experiences and draw together to heal and help each other. My hope is that the reader can also get a real feeling for the beauty and kindness in our communities. We have the tools to make good medicine, to make good families and make good decisions.

Thinking about it, the stories can also provide a layering of thoughts about women and the impact on us of colonization, and our susceptibility to other kinds of violence and to erasure.

To me, the stories represent freedom and the notion that we have stuff enough in us to get better. If we don't, someone else will.

Finally, I think there is a thread in this quilt about the blending of new and ancient knowledge.

How did you think of this character?

Oh, I love Bernice. I still cry over her quiet strength, hard choices and pain. My celebrations over her good choices, healing and gentleness in the face of exceptional violence are never-ending. What I think about her is different than what I feel. She lives such an internal life for the bulk of this work that I had the fear that readers would not "get" how deeply she thinks, experiences and feels.

She is an amalgam of every woman I love, have been challenged by and am.

How much of it is you?

Lots of it. None of it. It depends on the day. Bernice is more willing to love and trust at the end of her story than I think I am. She has the same reliance upon an almost unspoken and Creator-given right to the love of women that I think I share. She loves her aunties like I do: fully. However, I quite love my uncles. Almost without exception, they were gentle, compassionate and kind Cree men.

Her hurt, and her silence in her hurt, is familiar to me and can evoke a real pang in my heart, even today.

My hope is that in my best moments I am as lovely and kind as she is.

What lesson is there in this for parents? For children?

It is not enough to talk love, you have to live love. Loving means acting. Acting loving means making hard decisions about the safety – physical, sexual, emotional and spiritual safety – of your children. If you are unsure, do not let your children spend any time alone with any adult. If you are sure, ask yourself if you should be. Ever vigilant. Ever loving.

I hope some big buffalo of a gal in some small town (perhaps northern) pulls this book off a shelf when she is too young to see it. This is the book I wish I had found. Tell someone. Tell anyone. You have it inside you to be good, be well and get better.

Bernice gets skinny. Does she get well?
Well, she gets skinny and then she starts getting well. Skinny is not well in this book. Her Auntie Val is well. Maggie is not. Freda and Lola are somewhere in the middle. She comes into herself when she comes into her spirit, not when she comes into her body. She is sick in her skinniness, really, in the same way *Pimatisewin* is sick. She gets fed love as the tree gets fed love. She is better when fat with the love of women.

The book has a great deal of violence in it. Were you worried about how audiences would respond to it?
I was more worried that audiences could not relate to it – because not seeing it or knowing it exists makes it less understandable and sometimes more prevalent. At one point, one reader of an early draft said to me that sexual assault by multiple family members would be too hard for many readers to believe. In order to write this book, I had to write it for those of us who can believe it. Have experienced it. Have seen it. This is not to say that sexual assault is endemic to some communities and not others. I was worried about grounding this in an Indigenous context, that is true, because I feared that some readers would think that violence between adults and sexual violence against children by

adults would be seen to be an Indigenous issue. It is. It also is a non-Indigenous issue. When it happens to Indigenous peoples and when it happens to non-Indigenous peoples. Not talking about it, the degree, kind and prevalence, is the space within which the violence finds strength. Sexual assault may seem to be at the centre of Bernice's story, but it is not. Bernice's wellness and kindness is the centre of the story. The understanding that you can uncover and recover from sexual assault is important; knowing that you can make a healthy family, a healthy self and a "good life" is even more so.

The Pimatisewin *is a large part of this work. What does it represent, to Bernice?*
Loosely translated, *Pimatisewin* means "the good life." In this work, I have written it to represent a tree of life. In actuality, the tree itself represents that there is wellness, beauty and potential for regeneration through nature. That potentiality exists only if you take responsibility (in this book, making a blood offering to give life and a feast offering to give thanks). Metaphorically, it is a reminder that life is outside ourselves, that regardless of what is going on in our minds, our spirits and bodies have an obligation to our natural environment to behave in reciprocal, healing and positive ways. For Bernice, the tree represents her responsibility both to look outside of herself and take care of her relatives and others and to behave and make decisions in a way that will allow her to live a good life. Her commitment to personal health and the good life is important, but she cannot live a good life by continuing to concentrate only on self.

There is a Storyteller outside of the women in the book that comes in some chapters of the book. Whose voice is acimowin*?*

The Storyteller is the one who is recording Bernice's story, her oral history, in a way that it can teach others. When I started the work, I thought that it was an old man and pictured him telling the story in a way that tied *Pimatisewin*, Bernice and her family's lives together, years after they were gone, for people who needed to learn the lessons from a narrative and not a novel. If you read just those pieces alone, my hope is that you would understand the lessons she was taught. The Storyteller is entertaining, crass, an archivist and a lawbook author.

Closing thoughts for readers?

Look for the richness and joy, know that the pain exists, take responsibility for that which you create. I chose the name "Meetoos" from a number of names that resonated with me and from community members around me. When I told an Elder, she said, "You know that word means 'tree,' don't you?" I had no idea. My closing thought is prepare yourself for the possibility that you don't know all of the possibilities; grace and goodness can come just as fast and honestly as any other circumstance.